THE Horrible Bag of Terrible Things

ROB RENZETTI

PENGUIN WORKSHOP

PENGUIN WORKSHOP
An imprint of Penguin Random House LLC, New York

First published in the United States of America by Penguin Workshop,
an imprint of Penguin Random House LLC, New York, 2023

Text copyright © 2023 by Rob Renzetti
Illustrations copyright © 2023 by Penguin Random House LLC

Illustrations by M. S. Corley

Photo credit: Paper texture: Miodrag Kitanovic/iStock/Getty Images

Visit us online at penguinrandomhouse.com.

Library of Congress Cataloging-in-Publication Data is available.

Printed in the United States of America

ISBN 9780593519523

1st Printing

LSCC

Design by Mary Claire Cruz

FOR MY PARENTS, WHO SET ME ON THIS
JOURNEY. AND FOR MY WIFE, WHO HAS
MADE THE JOURNEY WORTHWHILE.

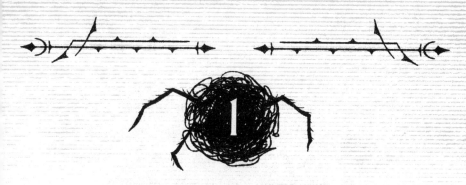

The Horrible Bag

THE BAG GROANED. When he lifted it off the front porch, he could have sworn that it groaned. He dropped the bag to the entryway floor and took a step back.

He listened closely for any further sounds. None came. He leaned closer to the bag. Still nothing. No more groans. Also, no shipping label. No name or address. Who'd delivered it to their house? Was it something his parents had ordered? There was no way to find out till they got home from work, and that wouldn't be for hours.

In the meantime, he was stuck inside the house with his big sister. Did she know something about this? He doubted it. And if there was any fun to be had with the bag, she would surely put an end to it. Sometimes she treated her baby brother like he was an actual baby.

Zenith Maelstrom was eleven going on twelve. And the "going on" couldn't go fast enough for him. He could not wait to grow up so everyone would stop bossing him around, especially his sister, Apogee. What he wouldn't give to be the older sibling.

Zenith took a step closer to the bag. It was the size of a small suitcase, but shaped like an old-fashioned doctor's satchel. It *felt* old. It looked exhausted. It slouched there on the floor, unable to stand upright. The bag had bad posture.

The bag had bad skin as well. Or more accurately, bad *skins*. It was made of several types of animal hide. Some patches had the smooth appearance of finished leather, while others looked as though they'd been stripped directly off some exotic beast, bristled hair and all. One section sported rough reptilian scales. The various pelts were sewn together with heavy, haphazard stitches. This rough-hewn exterior was adorned with an improbably elegant, but tarnished, brass clasp that ran the length of the bag's opening. It had been fashioned to resemble the vines of a rosebush. A few rosebuds nestled among many sharp thorns.

Bad skin. Bad posture. General air of hostility.

The bag reminded him of Kevin Churl, neighborhood braggart and one of Zenith's least favorite people. Had Kevin sent the bag to him? Was this some sort of revenge for what'd happened on the pond in Kalikov Park? Delivered almost a year and a half later? It was a long time to hold a grudge, but still . . . Zenith scratched the scar hidden under the hair above his left ear, then caught himself and stopped. He decided this wasn't Churl's style. If Kevin were going to leave something on his doorstep, it would probably be a dog turd inside a flaming paper sack.

A heavy moan sounded from the bag as its metal-rimmed mouth opened wide. Zenith grabbed his baseball bat from the corner and brandished it at the bag, waiting for whatever was inside to leap out.

Nothing leapt out. Whatever moaned must have been too tired to do any leaping. Or too hurt. Or too clever? Perhaps it was waiting for Zenith to stick his head into the opening so it could jump up and latch on to his face.

He decided to toss the bag back out the front door. Just as soon as he'd taken a quick look inside. He *had* to look inside. No doubt about that. His sister always said that Zenith was "as curious as a killed

cat." Apogee was clever, and unbeatable at most games and puzzles, but idioms often got the better of her.

Holding the bat in front of him, Zenith inched his way closer to the bag, leaned forward, and peered down inside. It was dark. He retreated and turned on the overhead light. He inched up on the bag again. Still dark. Darker than it should be with the light on. He stuck the bat into the bag and poked around, trying to rouse whatever might be lying coiled inside. All he found was the bottom and the four corners. He used the bat's knob to hook the bag's handle and shook it. Nothing. Doing exactly what he swore he wouldn't, he stuck his head into the opening. Nothing latched on to his face. Nothing happened. Because there was nothing in the bag.

He dropped it to the floor and returned his bat to the corner. He was relieved. And disappointed. It was a pretty poor practical joke, whoever had pulled it. Absentmindedly, Zenith went to close the clasp and nicked his finger on one of the thorns. Just a pinprick, but deep enough to draw blood, a single drop of which fell into the bag's open mouth.

Zenith let out a cry of pain.

The bag responded with a sigh of pleasure.

Zenith's eyes went wide. He scrambled backward till he hit the wall.

The bag snapped shut, straightened up, and shivered with delight. A change of color rippled across its various skins. The bag's entire surface became brighter. *Awake* was the word that popped into Zenith's head.

Slowly, the bag's mouth opened into a wide grin, and a terrible thing came crawling out.

The Terrible Thing

ZENITH SAT STUPEFIED as one spindly black leg rose up from inside the bag and settled onto the floor. Then a second spindly black leg emerged. Then a third. A fourth. And then a fifth. And although Zenith thought to himself, *Yes, I get the picture. You can stop right there,* out came legs six through nine.

Mercifully, the legs stopped multiplying. They held still for a moment. But then all nine of them lifted a loathsome body out of the bag's dark interior.

The creature looked like a coughed-up hairball come to life. Its black body was the size of a large, misshapen melon. There was no identifiable head. The tangled hair that covered its body was coated in thick, sticky-looking goo. Each leg consisted of a twisted black braid of this same stringy hair, with white flecks woven sporadically throughout. A larger group of the flecks had gathered at the bottom of each leg, where the hair was at its thinnest. Zenith thought they looked like square white pebbles in the toe of a threadbare sock, and only then realized what they actually were. The white flecks were toenails. Whole human toenails.

The thing took one tentative step forward, the toenails clicking as its leg touched the wood floor. Another more confident step followed, then another, and then—*skitter, skitter, skitter*—the creature ran toward Zenith at a frightening pace.

Zenith wanted it nowhere near him but was unable to move. His two legs (a pitiful number by comparison) were unable or unwilling to help him escape.

If the creature's aim was to attack him, it was wide of the mark. It slammed into the wall a foot to Zenith's right and stuck there, like a suction cup. It lifted two legs and pushed hard to free itself. The body slowly came away from the wall with a sickening *shluuuurrp . . . pop!* The creature was unprepared for its success, and stumbled backward toward the opposite wall. *Wham!* It hit and became stuck again. *Shluuuurp . . . Pop!* It came free and stumbled away,

but this time it gained control of itself and stopped in the center of the front hall.

Zenith tensed, anticipating another attack. But the creature scuttled away from him and down the long hallway, deeper into the house.

This was enough to get Zenith's own legs working again. He got up off the ground, grabbed the horrible bag, and ran down the hall in pursuit. He launched himself through the air, his arms and the upside-down bag leading the way. The bag came down on top of the thing as he landed with a loud thud and a long slide across the wood floor. Zenith came to rest in the large archway that opened onto the living room, in full view of his big sister.

Big Sister

LUCKILY, APOGEE WAS too immersed in the game on her phone to look up. She tapped furiously at the screen, scowling. The tip of her tongue protruded from between her lips. She hunkered down on the sofa with her shoes propped on the edge of the coffee table, her gangly legs bent at the knees and jittering with nervous energy. Apogee had always been short for her age, and although Zenith was two years younger, he'd been as tall as his sister until an annoying growth spurt a year and a half ago had added six inches to her height. Almost all of it had occurred in her legs, and Apogee still didn't know what to do with them.

Zenith quickly slid the upended bag up against the wall separating the hall from the living room so that it would be out of his sister's line of sight and got to his feet. Apogee shifted and sighed. "You're

making a lot of noise out there, Nit. Should I be taking my 'guard' duties more seriously?"

Two things instantly rankled Zenith. The nickname Nit, which he hated, and the fact that his sister had been assigned to keep an eye on him while he was grounded.

His spring semester had ended with a literal bang when Zenith's enthusiasm for chemistry had inspired a kitchen experiment with explosive results. His mother returned home from work at the vet's one Friday to discover black smoke wafting from the blender and putrid blue goo splattered across the cabinets. His efforts to clean up the mess before her return had only made matters worse; it turns out you *can* stain a stainless-steel oven. Despite all this, Zenith argued that his extracurricular project displayed initiative and intellectual curiosity, admirable traits that should be encouraged, if not rewarded. Instead, his exasperated parents grounded him for the first two weeks of summer vacation, appointing Apogee as his guardian and minder while they were both away at work.

His confinement was almost over, but if his parents found out that he'd released a nine-legged

monster inside the house? He might be grounded for the rest of the summer.

Apogee spoke again and looked up at him this time. "What sort of trouble are you getting into out there? You've got a face with guilt written all over it." She paused, and her voice softened. "Seriously, do you need my help?"

There was a time when he would've told her everything. A time when they would've solved this problem together. When they were "thick thieves" as Apogee had awkwardly put it. But then Apogee had turned thirteen, and in the year and a half since, she'd been thwarting his schemes instead of helping come up with them. And when she couldn't stop him, she would rat on him. Zenith had been hurt and confused. Weren't you supposed to get *more* rebellious in your teen years? Not Apogee. In place of his old co-conspirator, Zenith now had a third parent. The idea that Apogee would actually lend a hand in the midst of this monstrous crisis seemed impossible.

"Help with what?" Zenith responded in as innocent a voice as he could muster.

"With whatever's making your scar itch." Apogee looked at the space above his left ear, where Zenith

was nervously scratching. He cursed under his breath and stopped fidgeting. He'd hurt his head during the accident on the pond, needing seven stitches to close it back up. It was fully healed, but the scar still itched when he was stressed or feeling guilty, something his sharp-eyed sister had helpfully pointed out to their parents. Now it had roused Apogee's suspicion enough to get her off the couch and headed for the hall.

Zenith's eyes darted down to where he'd hidden the bag. It wasn't there. He detected movement in his peripheral vision, but he didn't dare turn his head. Instead, he lifted his eyes and stared straight ahead as his sister approached. He opened his mouth, hoping that his brain would get the hint and come up with something to stop her from entering the hallway and spotting the creature in the bag.

But Apogee let his brain off the hook. Instead of walking out into the hall, she leaned against the archway and launched into a lecture that he'd heard many times over the past couple of weeks. This was the speech where she started by sympathizing with him about being grounded at the start of the summer, and then segued quickly into how he deserved it for

being so reckless. Neither of them was really listening. Apogee because she knew this speech by heart,
and Zenith because he was panicked.

After scrutinizing his face rather intently for a few
moments, Apogee's eyes were drawn back down to
her phone, and Zenith decided to chance a glance
down the hallway.

The bag was about halfway down the corridor.
As he watched, the thing inside pushed the upside-
down bag up off the ground and propelled it forward
for a few feet before it dropped to the hardwood
floor. After a short rest, it was up again. It went a
little farther and dropped a little harder. As it rose
for a third time, Zenith rooted silently for the thing
to make it around the corner of the L-shaped hallway
before Apogee realized what was going on. Instead,
it smacked against the far wall, then collapsed again,
still in full view.

Zenith took two furtive steps to his left. Apogee
wrapped up her lecture, looked up from her phone,
and turned to face him, away from the thing at the
end of the hall.

There was an awkward silence as Apogee waited
for a response to the speech they both had ignored.

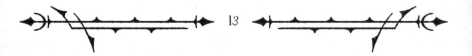

"Look, I'm sorry, okay," Zenith said, not sounding sorry at all. He cleared his throat and tried to sound more sincere. "I'm sorry if I'm making too much noise. I'll try to keep it down, I promise."

Apogee glared at him, eyebrows raised. "Yeah, you're definitely up to something." She turned back toward the living room and gestured for him to follow. "Come in here where I can keep an eye over you." Apogee walked back to the couch, but instead of following, Zenith took another look down the corridor.

"What's so interesting out there?" asked Apogee. Zenith turned to see his sister standing in front of the couch with her arms crossed; her eyes fixed him with a withering gaze.

"Nothing." He came into the living room and collapsed onto the couch.

Apogee apparently bought this answer, and why not? It had the advantage of being true. There *was* nothing in the hallway. The bag and the terrible thing inside it were gone.

Out of Sight

THEY SAT ON the sofa together, Apogee's eyes on her phone, Zenith's knees the ones now jittering with nervous energy.

"I'm hungry." Zenith stood up. "I'm going to go get a snack."

Apogee slid a small wooden bowl across the coffee table with her toe. "Nuts."

Zenith sat down. He put a pecan in his mouth. It lay on his tongue for a minute before he remembered to chew. He got up again. "I need to use the bathroom."

"No you don't."

He sat back down.

"Uhhhh," Zenith started, not knowing where his mouth might take him this time.

Apogee sighed with exasperation and dropped her phone. She shot him another of her scornful stares.

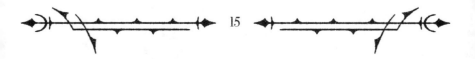

"I'm bored," he said. "Let me go get a comic book from my room. I'll be right back."

"I've got a better idea." Apogee reached over and opened the side table drawer. She slapped a deck of cards down in front of Zenith.

"Oh no," he said with dread.

"Oh yes," Apogee said with glee.

It was a simple card game from their childhood called Abundant Bunnies that Apogee had recently revived and revised into a winner-take-all battle with a monster theme. She'd skillfully drawn over the artwork, changing the sweet cottontail critters into zombunnies, wererabbits, and vampire rab-bats. Apogee was the only one who really understood the new rules, and thus won almost every game. Zenith's only chance to escape quickly would be to draw the black bunny that had been transformed into a black hole. This card instantly ended the contest, as it would suck up every other card on the table.

But before his sister had even finished shuffling, there was a clatter from the hallway.

Apogee perked up. "What was that?"

"What was what?" Zenith grabbed the cards and

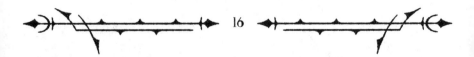

started to deal, suddenly very anxious to distract his sister with the game.

Apogee was up and moving toward the hall. "You didn't hear that?"

He followed her without answering. Should he come clean before Apogee found the terrible thing? Or was there a chance he could feign ignorance of the beast and get away with it?

"Zenith!" He cringed, then relaxed when he saw that Apogee was standing over his baseball bat, which had fallen over and hit the floor. She picked it up and handed it to him. "Keep your stuff in your room."

This was the break he needed. "You got it. I'll put it away right now." He hurried down the hall, doing his best to scan the shadowed corners without arousing Apogee's suspicion. Hopefully, she would return to the living room in his absence and give him some time to search for the intruder unimpeded.

Shlurp

ZENITH WAS SURPRISED to see the horrible bag sitting on his bedroom floor. To say he was *pleasantly* surprised would be stretching it. There was nothing pleasant about the bag, but he was grateful to have found it. Unfortunately, it was tipped over on its side and empty.

Yet there was no doubt that the thing from inside the bag was still in his bedroom. He could hear the unseen monster moving around, making that sick, sticky noise. *Shlurp. Shlurp.*

Without looking, Zenith reached behind himself and closed the bedroom door with the tip of his bat. He took a batter's stance and waited nervously.

The noises got louder. *Shlurp. Shlurp! SHLURP!* It sounded like the creature was near, but he couldn't see it anywhere. And then there was a *POP* from overhead. Zenith looked up to see the living hairball

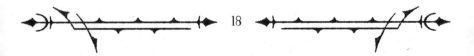

hanging from the ceiling light, its legs pulled together and stretched to three times their original length, allowing its awful body to dangle just over Zenith's head.

The terrible thing fell onto his face. His eyes, nose, and mouth were buried in the viscous, endless hair. The smell of spoiled milk flooded his nostrils. He dropped the bat and clutched at the thing. His fingers dug deep into the sticky web of tangled tresses and discovered something more solid. A beating heart hid at its center. His hands recoiled in disgust and the creature quickly slipped down off his face. Zenith's relief was brief. Panic returned as its nine legs coiled around his shoulders and torso, the toenails digging into his back. The creature slowly slid across his chest till its pounding heart was directly over his own. The wet, feverish warmth of it made him want to crawl out of his skin. He started to squirm, but the thing tightened its grip and pressed itself against him, its heartbeat growing more intense and erratic, as if the monster were sending out a plaintive call and listening desperately for a reply.

Then all at once, the beast detached itself and fell

to the floor. It lay there unmoving, its legs splayed beside its inert body.

Zenith put his hand on his chest and felt his own heart racing. Had he somehow killed the thing? With his heartbeat?

He picked up his bat, gently poked the beast, and leapt backward. There was no reaction. He came forward and poked it again, this time a little harder. Nothing. He pulled his arm back, then thrust the bat at the lump as if he were fencing with it. *Splurch!* He instinctively pulled the bat back before realizing the beast had gotten stuck to its tip. It was now inches from his face.

Zenith yelped and shook the bat rapidly, trying to dislodge the thing. When this didn't work, he cranked the bat back and swung hard. The creature came off, flew across the room, and thwacked against the miniature basketball net on the back of his closet door. The flimsy apparatus and the monster fell to the floor with a loud crash.

The bedroom door swung open, and Apogee rushed into the room. "Zenith! Are you okay?!" Her panicked gaze fell on Zenith's face for only a moment before she saw the horrible bag and hideous beast.

Her eyes widened, and her jaw slackened. She took a small step back. "Wh-what?"

Shlurp the hairball came back to life. A leg quickly slithered across the floor and wrapped itself around Apogee's ankles. She screamed in surprise as the creature pulled her off her feet and dragged her across the floor. Zenith watched in frozen terror as its other legs bound her arms to her body. Its body flattened and slid across her chest, listening to her heart the same way it'd listened to Zenith's. Hers must have been more to its liking. Shlurp's body shivered, and its color shimmered just as the bag had when his blood had dripped into its black maw.

One of Shlurp's legs unwound itself from Apogee's shoulders and shot across the floor into the tipped-over bag's open mouth. The creature tightened its hold on his sister, then pulled itself toward the opening, dragging Apogee along with it, headfirst. She gasped for breath and struggled to break free.

Zenith tried to scream and break his paralysis. "AaaAAAHH! Get off her!" He ran to them with his bat raised. He started to swing at Shlurp, but stopped himself before he connected. Hitting the creature's body would mean smashing his sister in

the chest. Instead, he tried striking the leg that was pulling them toward the bag, but it was like hitting a taut bungee cord. The bat merely bounced off and did nothing to slow Shlurp down.

Zenith lowered the bat and looked at Apogee, hoping she might have some idea how he could help her. Her eyes were wide with fright. The only word she uttered was his name.

"Zeni—"

And then her whole head was pulled inside the horrible bag. There was a slight pause, and Apogee's shoulders went in as well. Another pause, and her entire torso disappeared.

Zenith marveled. This was physically impossible. The bag was simply not that big. But the bag didn't seem to care. It swallowed up Apogee's thighs. Zenith grabbed her furiously kicking feet before the bag could complete its magic trick. He pulled as hard as he could, to no effect. "I've got you! Just . . . hold on!"

Apogee's feet were yanked out of his hands, leaving only one sneaker behind. The force of the action flipped the bag so that it sat upright. Its mouth snapped shut. The bag stretched upward as

a shimmer ran across its surface. Then it collapsed and darkened.

Zenith dropped the orphaned shoe, bent over, and grabbed the bag. He was determined to force it open. But no force was necessary. The bag came open easily.

It was empty.

Alone

WITHOUT THINKING, ZENITH thrust his hand into the bag, running it along the bottom, back and forth, searching every inch. There was nothing unusual. No secret compartments, no hidden depths. He lifted the bag up and examined the floor beneath it. No trapdoors. Just his plain old bedroom floor.

Had he really expected to find secret compartments and trapdoors? Did he think that Apogee had set up an elaborate practical joke with a trick bag? *He'd* been the one that had brought the bag into their home. And *he'd* unleashed the thing that had taken her away.

He looked at his digital clock. His parents wouldn't be home for another two hours. Even if he called them and confessed everything right now, it would take them at least a half hour to drive home. *If*

they believed him. The same *if* applied to any neighbor or friend he went to for help. How long would it take to convince someone he wasn't kidding or crazy? And what would happen to Apogee in the meantime?

If only his big sister were here to tell him what to do. But he knew what he had to do, and knew he had to do it alone. "My sister's been taken, and it's up to me to get her back." Zenith said this out loud, to make it more real, perhaps. To solidify it. Because inside he felt anything but solid. His mind was abuzz with panic and fear, searching frantically for solutions. He knew nothing about this bag except for what he'd seen with his own eyes, and what he'd seen defied all logic.

Zenith noticed the afternoon sunlight glinting off the metal latch. There *was* one thing he knew about the bag that might help him. It liked the taste of his blood.

Zenith opened the bag and pressed a fresh finger to the tarnished brass thorn that had pricked him earlier. He held his hand over the bag and offered it another drop of his blood.

The moan was louder this time. The bag snapped

shut and stretched skyward as it had before, its color brightening before its mouth opened wide.

Zenith hoped that, like any good magician at the conclusion of an illusion, the bag would make his sister reappear. But he knew that rule would not apply. This wasn't stage magic.

The bag sat there with its mouth agape, waiting for whatever came next.

"You know what comes next," snarled Zenith. He was suddenly angry as well as scared. He tightened the laces on his grubby green sneakers and zipped up his navy-blue hoodie. He grabbed his backpack off the bed. It was heavier than usual. He'd been planning to go on an epic exploration of their neighborhood as soon as he was ungrounded and had already packed it with snacks and water. His preparation was coming in handy now. Zenith shoved Apogee's shoe inside his pack without looking and slung it over his shoulder. He strode purposely over to the bag and peered down inside.

It was too dark to see anything, but he sensed a large space opening up below him. It was as though he was gazing down into a deep well. Zenith raised one foot above the bag and then very slowly lowered

it into its mouth. The air was much cooler inside the bag than in his bedroom. He felt around with his foot, but found nothing. He kneeled on the bedroom floor and lowered the entire length of his leg into the bag, but he still found nothing solid on which to plant his foot.

Zenith grabbed one side of the bag's opening, half expecting it to slam shut and bite his hand. But it remained rigidly open, as though it had locked itself in place. Another trick, probably. "This may be the worst decision I've ever made in my entire life," he announced. If Apogee had been there, she would definitely have had something to say about that. But the bag expressed no opinion.

Zenith tightened his grip with both hands, being careful to avoid the clasp's thorns, swung his remaining leg over the lip of the bag, and lowered the rest of his body into its dark depths.

Foul Mouths

THE OPENING EXPANDED around Zenith as he lowered himself into the horrible bag. The brass clasp grew in his hands, his fingers sliding across its surface and coming to rest around the convex shape of one of its now gigantic vines. Zenith tightened his grip and tensed his arms as the rapid growth of the bag came to an abrupt stop.

Zenith hung from his hands inside the now cavernous interior. The light from his bedroom illuminated the huge brass clasp, at either end of which he could see enormous hinges affixed to the animal hides with dense knots of stitching. The stitches formed seams that traced the length of the bag's angled ceiling before sloping down and disappearing into the darkness. The dim light only reached so far. The expanse beneath him was a murky mystery.

But it wouldn't remain a mystery for long. His hands were slowly slipping on the smooth surface of the brass vine. Soon he would lose his grip and find out what was below, in the most painful way possible. He was tempted to climb back out of the bag. But then what would become of Apogee?

As Zenith's eyes adjusted to the dark, he spotted a loose length of thread dangling to his left. It was the size of the climbing rope from gym class. This was something he could keep a firm grip on, if he didn't slip and fall getting over to it. He would definitely fall if he stayed where he was.

He took a deep breath and began traversing hand over hand across the brass clasp toward the thread. The clasp's vine ran all the way to the end, and he was able to use several of its thorns as handholds. His legs began to swing wildly in counterpoint to his arms as he traveled. If he paused when he reached the end of the clasp, would the momentum of his lower body cause him to fly off into the abyss?

Better not to find out. Zenith increased his speed as he approached the end and simply kept going. His front hand swung out into nothing. The hand behind his head lost its grip on the brass vine. He sailed

through the air, arm outstretched, fingers straining. He began to drop.

But as he did, his hand closed around the dangling thread. Pain flared as his palm slid quickly down its rough surface. Zenith gritted his teeth, tightened his grip, and grasped the thread with his other hand. A moment later both his legs were twined tightly around it.

The thread swung forward as Zenith clung to it. There was a short *snap*, and he abruptly dropped as the seam popped a stitch. He swung back, swung forward again, and—*snap*—popped another stitch. Then another and another as the seam unraveled and Zenith fell downward into the darkness. The thread reached the end of its seam and stopped unraveling, but Zenith kept going. He swung up and hit the side of the bag, grabbing on to one ridge and planting his feet on another while maintaining his hold on the thread.

Zenith peered down the length of the wall. The ridges looked like the snake scales he'd noticed on the bag's exterior, but each of these scales was the size of a kite. *Snakeskin doesn't have scales on both sides,* thought Zenith, and then realized he was

looking for logic while clinging to the interior wall of a giant doctor's bag that'd conspired with a hairball to kidnap his sister. He looped the end of the thread around the edge of a scale and climbed down. He reached the bottom and looked around. The dim light from the opening above did almost nothing to illuminate the bag's base. There was plenty of darkness for Shlurp to hide in.

Zenith moved toward the center of the bag, whispering, "Apogee?" with every other step.

From somewhere up ahead, a voice whispered back. "Over here!"

He moved more quickly. "Apogee? Is that you?" He took another twenty steps.

"Back here."

How'd he passed her? He retraced his steps. "Am I closer?" he asked.

"You've missed me again." The voice giggled.

He moved slowly to his right. He was getting frustrated with this game. "Apogee! Stop fooling around."

"Who's Apogee?" the voice asked from directly below him.

Zenith looked down. He screamed and scrambled

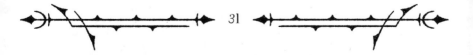

back, losing his balance and falling on his backside. There was a seam running between his legs, and a two-foot section without stitches opened and closed as it spoke to him.

"Well, don't just sit there," scolded the mouth in the floor. "I asked you a question. Who is Apogee?"

He stood up and backed farther away. The mouth made no effort to follow him. *Could* it follow him? Regardless, it wasn't attacking him, and that was a vast improvement over Shlurp, the previous surprise the horrible bag had coughed up.

He took a tiny step toward the mouth. "Um, Apogee is my sister."

"Speak up and speak clearly."

Zenith cleared his throat and straightened his back. "I said, she's my sister. She was grabbed by this, uh, spider-hairball thing and dragged inside this bag."

"*Bag?* What is this *bag* you speak of?"

Zenith was confused. "The bag we're inside of. The bag you're a part of." He gestured around with his arms. "Can't you see where you are?"

"Don't ask silly questions, young fool. I have no eyes. How am I supposed to see anything?"

"You don't have ears either," responded Zenith, losing his fear and gaining some anger. "So how are you hearing me?"

"Don't waste your time talking with her," another voice said. It, too, was feminine, but deeper and gruffer than the first one. Zenith turned around and saw another, larger opening in the seam. "She enjoys toying with strangers. I'll tell you about your sister."

"You saw her? Er, I mean, you know where she is?"

"Well, I know where she went," answered the big mouth. "She was taken to GrahBhag."

"GrahBhag? Where is GrahBhag?"

"More silly questions," snickered the little mouth.

"Quiet!" commanded Big Mouth. And then in a more comforting tone, she explained, "GrahBhag is the land that lies beyond this place. Your sister passed through to GrahBhag just a short time ago. If you hurry, I'm sure you can catch up with her."

"Can you show me the way?"

Big Mouth chuckled. "Why, my dear boy, I *am* the way. You need only slip through me, and you will be in GrahBhag."

As strange as it sounded, it was far from the strangest thing that'd happened that day. Zenith

tightened the straps on his backpack, took a step to-ward Big Mouth, and leaned forward to get a look inside.

"Ah-ah-ah! Not yet. First, we have some business to conduct," she said. "There is a small price for your passage."

Zenith patted his pants and cursed quietly. In his haste to go after Apogee, he'd left what little cash he had on top of his dresser. He sheepishly replied, "I have no money."

"Money? Now, what would I do with money?" asked Big Mouth. "Do you see any pockets on me?" Little Mouth giggled again. "You need not worry about money," continued Big Mouth. "You have my preferred method of payment on you. Or rather, within you."

"Do I need to answer three riddles or something?"

Little Mouth and Big Mouth both laughed at that. "No, no, no," said Big Mouth. "We've already seen that you don't handle questions very well, haven't we? No, I don't need you to use your mouth or your brain. I just need what's inside your veins."

Zenith was silent for a moment, then examined his sore fingertip. "You . . . need . . ."

"Blood, my dear boy," replied Big Mouth. "I need your blood."

Zenith turned white. "How much?"

"How much do you have?"

Zenith was speechless.

Big Mouth chuckled again. "Forgive me, but you *are* gullible, aren't you? I only require a small amount. Shall we say . . . five drops?"

"Three drops," Little Mouth chimed in. "I'll let you pass through me for only three drops of blood."

"Quiet!" roared Big Mouth. Her voice was all menace for a moment before she again assumed a friendlier tone. "Young man, the trip I am offering you for five drops is superior to my younger sister's offer in every way. GrahBhag is a strange and dangerous place filled with all manner of creature, both fair and foul. I will make sure that you are transported to a safe location in the very center of GrahBhag."

Little Mouth scoffed. "You're more likely to end up in the middle of the Desert of Despair. Or splash down in the middle of the Scalding Sea. For a mere three drops, I will deliver you to the loveliest little hilltop with the most charming view. I'm sure you'll be able to spot your sister from there."

"Liar!" thundered Big Mouth. "The moment she has your blood, she'll drop you in the Boiling Bog and be done with you!"

"You're the one who's lying, you old rip!"

"They're both lying," said a small, raspy voice from a corner near the wall of scales.

"Keep out of this," snarled Big.

"Mind your own business!" hissed Little.

A hint of desperation entered Big Mouth's voice as she continued her pitch. "All right, I'll match my sister's offer. Only three drops. Three drops will deliver you to a majestic summit on the outskirts of the capital city." Zenith ignored her and walked toward the corner.

There was a third opening in the same seam. This one was the smallest and most ragged looking. "I'm fairly certain that you've already paid for your trip. The drops of blood that fell from above were yours, were they not?"

"Yes."

"Well, then those two gluttons have had more than enough. You should have seen them, greedily slurping up the whole pool of it. And as usual they left nothing for me!"

"It's not our fault you were born in that dusty corner, Squirt," snickered Little Mouth, and she shared a laugh with her older sister.

"They think that nickname is clever because I'm always so parched. But I wouldn't be so thirsty if they ever shared!" Her sisters cackled even louder. "Anyway," she continued, "you've paid the price, and you can pass through whichever of us you prefer."

"Watch out for our youngest sister," warned Big Mouth. "She may seem humble, generous, and oh so sincere, but she is a viper. She asks for no blood up front because she will take it all once you step inside. Blood, bone, and gristle. She will grind you into a pulp."

"Do you see any teeth?" asked Dry Mouth, opening wide. Even in the dim light, Zenith could see she had none. "But by all means, feel free to squander some extra blood on my sisters' empty promises if it makes you feel more secure."

"Come now, my dear boy," purred Big Mouth. "For a small additional fee, you can travel with me to a fabulous destination in true style."

"I promise an experience that is second to none," countered Little Mouth.

"More lies," sighed Dry Mouth. "We all open up within a few feet of each other on a dusty hill-top overlooking Whichway Woods. The trip takes no more than a few seconds."

"You're just jealous, you jagged snag," hissed Little Mouth. "Why don't you sew yourself up and end your miserable existence?"

"No, I think I'll stick around just to spite you."

Zenith mulled things over as the three sisters continued to bicker. He sympathized with Dry Mouth, perhaps because her plight reminded him of his own—at a disadvantage because she was younger and saddled with an annoying nickname. He took a step closer to the mouth in the corner.

Big Mouth cried out, "Don't do it, you fool! She's not to be trusted."

"I'm guessing none of you are," Zenith said. "But she's the only one not trying to sell me on her services. Also, she's not asking for my blood. And all other things being equal, I'd like to hang on to as much of it as possible."

"All right, now," said Dry Mouth. "I'll hold my-self open, and you just climb in. Before you know it, you'll find yourself in GrahBhag. Pay no attention to anything my sisters shriek at you."

Her sisters did indeed scream some very nasty things as Zenith climbed into Dry Mouth's ragged opening. He quickly lost his footing and found himself falling down a dark, deep tunnel.

Distress

ZENITH TUMBLED END over end down the tunnel before suddenly, illogically, falling *up* and toppling out of a hole on a dusty hillside. He waited a moment for his brain and inner ear to catch up with what his eyes were telling him, then he stood and brushed himself off.

The hole from which he'd emerged was about the same size as Dry Mouth. A raggedly stitched seam ran between it and two larger holes nearby—a mirror image of the foul mouths inside the horrible bag. He half expected the holes to resume the sisters' cursing, but these doppelgangers appeared to be lifeless. The hillside was covered in the bag's scales on one side of the stitch and by its leathery hide on the other, but the scales were smaller than those he'd clutched during his descent into the bag, and the hide here was bleached by the sun. The sun itself appeared redder

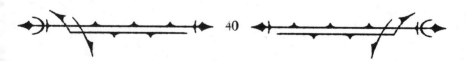

and dimmer than the one back home, and the sky was a sickly, pale green. Zenith favored green in his footwear, but didn't care for it as a sky color. It gave the atmosphere a stale feeling, like the whole world had exceeded its expiration date. This impression was strengthened by a sour scent in the air. Zenith felt a little queasy.

He shook his head to clear it and took another look around. Just a few feet behind him, beyond the three mouth holes, was a steep cliff. The sound of waves breaking on a distant beach came from that direction. Before him, the stitches wound their way down a gently sloping hill toward a dense forest.

Had Shlurp jumped off the cliff with his sister, diving into the water below? Had it flown? Or had it dragged her into the forest at the bottom of the hill?

A short, strangled scream from the woods provided his answer. Zenith cried out, "Apogee!" and ran down the hill. He gained speed quickly. Too quickly. When he tried to slow down, he slid down instead. He lost his balance, fell on his butt, and tumbled till he rolled to a stop at the bottom of the hill. Zenith stood up and glanced back at the hillside.

The stitches, skin, and scales on the hill's lower half were all covered by a dewy, dark green moss.

Zenith turned his attention to the forest before him. It had appeared so small and navigable from above, but now seemed unfathomably large. Botany was not Zenith's strong suit, but even his untrained eye could pick out a dozen different species of trees, all of which were intermingled in a way that looked both chaotic and combative. The trees were entangled and entwined, fighting for sunlight and space. The bushes' branches were twisted inward. More of the dark green moss blanketed the ground, making the forest floor slippery and treacherous. Zenith wasn't exactly eager to enter such a hostile-looking environment, but his sister was somewhere inside. He tightened the straps of his backpack and followed a narrow, moss-free stone path into the woods.

He called out, "Apogee? Apogee! Can you hear me? It's Zenith! Apogee?" He repeated this every few seconds, then every few minutes, and finally fell silent. The forest grew even more dense and foreboding. The air became thick and damp, and a rotten aroma permeated the place. It occurred to Zenith

that, before he found his sister, something foul might find him. "APOGEE!" he shouted, trying to drown out nasty thoughts of nasty things.

Zenith heard an anguished cry up ahead and quickened his pace. "Apogee," he called again, but the only reply was the sudden sound of rushing water. He slowed slightly. Little Mouth had tried to fool him once already by mimicking his sister. Was he now being tricked by a duplicitous waterfall? In this world, anything seemed possible.

He broke through some brush and came to a stop beside a swiftly flowing stream. Apogee was less than ten paces away. She lay on her stomach with her arms clutching the trunk of a tree at the edge of the water. Her ankles were still bound together by one of Shlurp's elastic legs, while the vile thing used the other eight to scramble frantically on the mossy ground, straining to find enough traction to break Apogee's hold on the tree.

Apogee lifted her head, her angry expression turning to one of worry as she spotted her brother. "Zenith! Stay back!"

Shlurp took advantage of her momentary distraction to yank her backward. She lost her grip on the

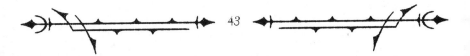

trunk and her chin hit the forest floor. But before the thing could drag her any farther, Apogee grabbed a loose root of the same tree. Or did the root grab on to her? It was suddenly wrapped around both her wrists, and Zenith had no idea how that'd happened. How had any of this happened? How had he found himself here, watching his sister play the role of the rope in a tug-of-war between a tree root and a living hairball?

Zenith shook his head to clear these useless musings and rushed forward.

"Zenith . . . NO! It's not . . . safe." As Shlurp tried to pull her free of the tree root, Apogee strained and struggled, slowly turning herself from her stomach onto her back. "I'm not . . . some distressed damsel . . . who needs . . . to be saved!" Apogee jerked her legs up, pulling Shlurp with them and slamming the creature into the tree trunk. One, two, three times. Then she brought them back down fast and the creature flew from her legs, bounced once, and landed upside down. Shlurp's nine legs scrambled furiously, but before it could right itself, Zenith ran forward, wound up, and kicked the terrible thing into the rushing stream. As he watched the churning

water carry Shlurp away, he heard his sister come up behind him.

"Nice kick, Nit," she said as she elbowed his arm. Zenith opened his backpack and handed Apogee her missing shoe. "Thanks. Now let's get the heck out of here. That thing is bound to come back."

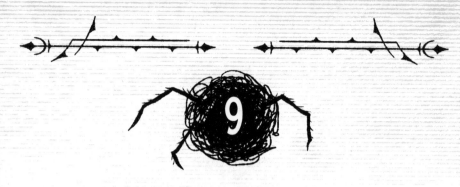

Whichway

THE TWO OF them walked briskly through the woods as Apogee, just as briskly, peppered her younger brother with questions about how they'd ended up in the world of GrahBhag. Zenith's father had pioneered this rapid-fire interrogation technique, but his mother and sister had perfected it. Apogee liked to say it kept Zenith's "tales from getting too tall," but Zenith still strived, whenever possible, to portray himself as an innocent victim of circumstance. It rarely got him off the hook, but it did tend to lessen his punishment. And he still hoped that they might escape this current misadventure without their parents finding out. *If* he and Apogee could return home first. And *if*, with the proper bribe, he could keep Apogee quiet about the day's inexplicable events. She certainly wasn't keeping quiet about any of it at the moment.

"And why did you open up the bag?" demanded Apogee. "Or even bring it into our home in the first place? I'm sorry to rake the coals over you, Nit, but you should know better than to mess around with something so dangerous."

"How was I supposed to know it was dangerous?"

"C'mon! You've got a nose for trouble, and we both know it." Did Zenith hear a hint of admiration in her voice? "The problem is that you like the scent!"

"Let's talk about *your* nose and how you like to stick it in where it doesn't belong. Always meddling in things, bossing me around, stopping anything fun."

"Someone's got to keep you from getting killed," scolded Apogee. "If I hadn't 'meddled' in your rooftop stargazing this spring, you and your telescope would've *both* fallen and been smashed on the driveway. And what about back in January? You'd have been buried alive under your own collapsed snow fort."

"Our house is one story, Apogee. I've fallen off the roof before and survived. The only reason my telescope didn't survive is because *you* startled me by popping out of your bedroom window, so I dropped the thing. And *you* made my fort collapse by dragging me out of it! You conveniently forgot those details, didn't you?"

Apogee scoffed. *"I'm* the one revising history? If you'll reme . . ." Her voice suddenly failed, and her eyes went wide.

They'd come to the edge of a large clearing. Zenith's spirits lifted slightly at the sight of the open sky, but its olive-green color confused him. Did this color indicate sunset? Something told him that they'd better hurry if they wanted to be out of the woods and back home before nightfall.

And yet Zenith remained still. The geometric symmetry of the clearing was in stark contrast to the chaotic woods that surrounded it. The stone path they were now on stretched out before them in a straight line across the open space. An identical-looking perpendicular path ran from left to right and bisected their own in the center of the clearing. The intersection of the two paths was occupied by a large circular stone. Four granite columns, approximately eight feet tall, were placed around the clearing's edge in the empty spaces between the paths. And atop the four columns were perched four gargoyles, their bodies hunched and claws extended. Drool poured down

from their fanged mouths. Hungry eyes glowed and glowered at them from dark sockets. Zenith flinched at the sight of them, but then realized they were made of stone. The late afternoon's slanting shafts of light created the glow on their eyes and made the moss around their mouths shimmer like saliva. They were only statuary. Zenith was certain of it.

Apogee whispered, "The vibes in this place are bad." She grabbed her brother's hand and tried to pull him back into the woods, but Zenith stood firm and jerked his hand free.

"It's just a clearing with some funky statues," he insisted. "We don't have time to go around." He hurried forward, keeping his eyes focused on the path in front of him.

Apogee hissed, "Zenith!" But when he kept going, she reluctantly followed.

She caught up to him as he reached the center of the clearing, and they stepped onto the central stone together. It started to spin in place like a top. Zenith and Apogee smacked into each other and fell to their hands and knees, clutching the stone to avoid being thrown off, even as it increased its speed. Only after a stomach-churning minute of frantic rotation did it begin to slow down. But when it finally stopped spinning, their heads did not. It took Zenith three tries to get up on his feet and off of the trick rock. Apogee just scooted backward till she was free of it. When Zenith's vision was clear enough to survey their surroundings, he no longer had any idea which way he was facing, or which path was theirs. The clearing's strict symmetrical layout, the columns, and stone walkways all seemed quite sinister now.

"Which way, Nit?" Apogee asked, anxiety creeping into her voice. Zenith looked up at the darkening sky, then back down at the four possible ways forward. The gargoyles had been looking toward them when they stood on the edge of the clearing. Their eye direction should have pointed back to the way from which they'd come, but through some trick of the skilled sculptor, the eyes of the four stone figures had followed them to the center of the clearing. An absurd thought popped into his head—maybe one of the gargoyles would helpfully raise its arm and point to the correct path. But was this really any more absurd than a giant stone that spun you around like you were playing pin the tail on the donkey at the world's creepiest birthday party?

Zenith spotted a few leaves on the ground where one of the paths emerged from the forest. He pointed them out to Apogee and tried to sound confident. "One of us must have brushed up against a bush and knocked those to the ground as we entered the clearing." He marched in the opposite direction, away from the fallen leaves.

"But there are leaves all over the ground on all sides of us."

Zenith continued walking. Apogee was right, but he had nothing else to go on. They needed to keep moving. They needed to get out of the forest.

The Campsite

THEY DID NOT get out of the forest. Hours passed as they trudged onward. The maroon sun abandoned them, and the sky it left behind turned from olive to black. There was no moon, and the small smattering of stars did little to illuminate the forest floor. The siblings tried to find their way as best they could, but it was slow going. They walked close together, but in silence. Neither felt much like talking.

It turned out the spinning stone was just the first of many cruel tricks Whichway Woods had in store for them. The limbs of a majestic elm snatched Zenith's backpack and flung it into a dense bush. When he went to retrieve it, the bush wrapped its thorny branches around his arm and tried to pull him in. A babbling brook sprayed water at them with the force of a fire hose. Jagged rocks sprang up from

a previously level trail to trip Apogee, and she almost blundered into a deep pit. It was too dark to see the bottom, but as the two of them peered over the edge, they sensed that there was something coiled down there, waiting. The woods seemed to be filled with unseen somethings, either silently watching or promising further misfortune in voices low and gruff.

They were cold, wet, bruised, beaten, hungry, thirsty, and lost. *And aimlessly wandering,* thought Zenith. He stopped and sat down cautiously on a large rock. After all they'd endured, he wouldn't have been surprised if the rock had suddenly launched him into the sky like an ejector seat from those sixties spy movies he liked. But, at least for the time being, the rock behaved like a normal rock. Apogee let out a long sigh and slumped down beside him.

Zenith removed his backpack. Without a moment's respite from the perils of the forest, they hadn't yet inventoried its contents, but he had little hope that it contained any snacks or water. He'd been wearing the pack for hours, and the shape and weight of its contents hadn't felt right. He unzipped the smaller pocket first, and discovered a ballpoint pen and a half pack of gum that he couldn't remember

buying. He offered a stick to his sister. "Dinner is served." He unwrapped a second piece for himself. They chewed in silence for a moment, then Zenith dug into the larger pocket and pulled out his sister's physics book.

"Oh, crap." Zenith chuckled. "This has got to be the *tenth* time I've grabbed *your* backpack from the kitchen instead of mine." He slid the book back inside. "No wonder it's so heavy. Here, you can have it back." He playfully passed the backpack to his sister.

Apogee stifled a laugh and passed it back. "No way. It's your mistake. Consider it punishment for buying the same backpack as me."

"It's not the same at all! Sure, it's the same color, but the straps and zippers are completely different." Zenith smiled broadly. This was one argument with his sister that he always enjoyed.

"And yet you keep getting the two of them mixed up." Apogee grinned.

"Besides, I didn't buy it. Mom did." The smile disappeared from Zenith's face. "What do you think Mom and Dad are doing?"

"Freaking out," replied Apogee as her own smile

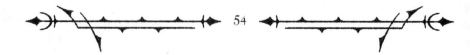

faded. "Searching the neighborhood. Calling the police."

"Will the police do anything if you're missing for less than forty-eight hours?"

"I don't think that waiting period applies to kids, Nit."

"Like you're an expert in police procedure." Something else occurred to him. "What if they take the bag to the cops? Are we going to come out in some police evidence locker? Will we still be able to get out at all? Or will the connection between the two worlds be broken?"

"I'm sure we'll be fine. We'll get out of the bag. But we might need to wait till morning to find our way."

"Oh, I guess you're an expert in bagworld rules now," muttered Zenith. And then they both fell silent again.

Zenith looked down at the dark ground for a long time, lost in his dark thoughts. When he looked up again, the dark woods were a little less dark. There was a faint, flickering glow coming from somewhere in front of them. Apogee noticed it as well.

Apogee whispered, "Go slowly. If we show too much interest, the forest will find some way to stop

us." Zenith nodded. His sister was showing a little of her old sneaky streak. He liked it. She got up and meandered in the general direction of the glow. Zenith did the same, stopping several times to gaze in the wrong direction and wander down divergent paths.

After an hour of painfully slow progress, they found themselves peering through some bushes at an odd campsite illuminated by firelight. Beyond the fire they could see a solitary tent, beside which was a turkey-like bird strung up by its feet with a rough rope. It appeared to be dead, but was still intact.

None of this was particularly strange. What *was* strange was the eight-foot-tall patchwork doll that someone had placed by the campfire. It was posed sitting on a log, elbows on knees, with its black button eyes staring at the flames. Other buttons formed a frowning mouth, while still more ran down the front of its torso, as if it were wearing a suit coat instead of a collection of mismatched rags.

"You think it's meant to scare away other creatures while the camper sleeps?" asked Apogee quietly.

"If only we'd had one of those things on our last camping trip," said Zenith.

"That bear came into our camp because you left a bunch of food out. I doubt a giant rag doll would've scared it away."

Zenith ignored this last comment. "The tent looks empty to me, but it's hard to tell from here. I'll get a closer look." He crept forward, but Apogee grabbed his hand and pulled him back.

"Stop!" she hissed. "We don't need any more surprises. Didn't the spinning stone teach you anything?"

"Yes. It taught me that this forest is never going to let us leave! We need food. We need water. And most of all we need help! Whoever's camp this is knows how to survive in these woods. *We* do not."

"And why would they help us?" Apogee tightened her grip on Zenith's arm. "Has anything in this world helped us so far?"

Zenith didn't have an answer. Actually, he did have an answer, and it was "no," but that didn't help his case. Maybe Apogee was right.

"Please, Zenith. We'll figure this out on our own. Don't go looking for help from some unseen stranger. You're too smart to be so stupid."

Zenith angrily yanked his arm free and burst out

from behind the bushes before Apogee could stop him. He strode briskly toward the campfire.

The patchwork man arose from his seat and turned to face him, shadow and firelight flickering across his massive frame. The behemoth reached for him with his mitten-shaped hand. His buttoned-up mouth emitted angry, strangled noises. Zenith staggered backward; his eyes locked on to the giant doll while his mouth made panicked, incoherent noises of its own.

Apogee had no problem speaking. "Run!"

And this time, Zenith listened to her. He ran back toward his sister, but the bushes rose up and bared their thorns. Apogee beat them back down and pushed them apart. The branches clutched and scraped at her, but she kept a space clear until Zenith was able to dive through the opening. He hit the ground and got to his feet quickly. The foliage stopped fighting with Apogee. Instead, the branches parted like a curtain as the living doll came forward with long strides of his boneless legs.

Zenith and Apogee ran. Rocks rose up in their path. Branches battered at them. They dodged the attacks, but the effort slowed them down. And they

heard the patchwork man close behind them, the guttural noises he made getting louder and more urgent.

They stopped abruptly on a narrow strip of ground at the foot of a tall waterfall. Water rushed past them and disappeared a hundred yards farther downstream over the lip of another, larger waterfall. There was nowhere left to run except for the way they'd come, and they could hear the giant rag doll approaching rapidly from that direction. Zenith looked back and forth desperately. Apogee bumped into him as she stepped away from the water.

"Watch it," he barked.

"Zenith. There's something in the river."

He turned to face her. "What?"

Apogee pointed at the water. It looked more like oil, murky and black.

Zenith squinted. She was right. Beneath the dark surface, something darker was lurking.

An explosive spray of water doused Zenith as the something sprang from the river. Shlurp leapt through the air and wrapped its nine legs around Apogee, trapping her arms against her sides. She yelped and blundered back, pulling her left arm free. Apogee punched Shlurp's soggy, squishy body. It

just tightened its grip, then sent one leg out into the stream, latching on to a large rock in the center. The beast yanked Apogee down into the water.

Zenith held his breath as his sister was pulled under and stayed under for what felt like forever before resurfacing a few yards away. He watched helplessly as the churning water carried Apogee and Shlurp downstream and then out of sight over the edge of the waterfall.

Before he had a moment to think, the rag doll man burst through the bushes, his guttural cries at a fever pitch. Zenith rubbed his scar furiously and growled with frustration and fear. He looked at the torrent and then once more at the towering rag man lumbering forward, his knitted hands straining toward Zenith's neck.

Zenith dove into the rapids. He was a strong swimmer, but not strong enough. The river swallowed him and spat him back up, turned him this way and that. It tossed him over the edge of the falls, and Zenith plummeted into the unknown.

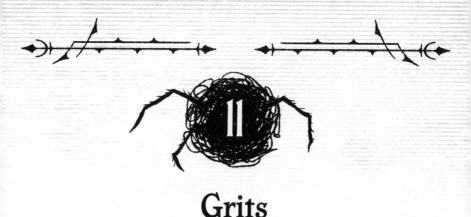

Grits

ZENITH WAS RUNNING with all his might. No, not running. Skating. He was skating with all his might on the frozen pond in Kalikov Park. He was skating for the goal. The winning goal. Kevin Churl was after him, but there was no way he would catch Zenith in time.

"Zenith! No!" someone cried out from the sidelines. He turned his head to look and saw Apogee. Why didn't she want him to win?

Kevin Churl tripped him with his hockey stick, and now he was on his back on the ice with Churl on top of him. The jerk had him pinned down, with his knees on Zenith's arms. Zenith couldn't get up or defend himself. Churl just sat on top of him laughing. Laughing, but with Apogee's voice. He was eating something while he laughed. Zenith tried to raise his head to see what the other boy was chewing on,

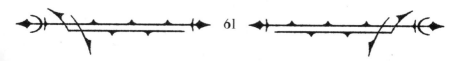

but his head would not move. He couldn't move at all. Churl was getting heavier. His laughter more intense. The chomping louder and louder!

Zenith's eyes shot open. He was on his back, looking up at the top of the trees. As best he could tell, the mint-green tint of the sky meant it was morning. He could hear the water, but thankfully he was no longer in it. He was nowhere near Kalikov Park or Kevin Churl. But something was on top of him.

He raised his head and shoulders. His feet were bare, and his shirt was pulled up. He decided he must still be dreaming, because the gargoyle statues from the clearing had come to life and apparently decided to make a meal of him. Three gargoyles held his feet as they dug under his toenails with long forefingers and nibbled on their harvest. The fourth gargoyle sat on his stomach and rooted around in his belly button. The force of its finger against his flesh convinced him this was all real.

Zenith greeted them with an earsplitting "Aaaaaggghhhhhh!" He sat up all the way and kicked his legs wildly. The startled creatures scampered a short distance, then froze in place. They hunched their backs, opened their mouths to mimic

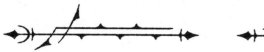

screaming, and transformed into stone.

Zenith was dumbfounded for a minute by this otherworldly version of playing possum. His soggy shoes were within arm's reach, so he grabbed one and chucked it at them. It bonked the largest gargoyle's head. "Get out of here!"

The outermost layer of stone "skin" covering each gargoyle burst into a cloud of gray dust, revealing the living creature beneath. Three of them disappeared into the nearest bush, but the smallest one stopped short and looked back at Zenith wistfully.

"What?" yelled Zenith. "You upset I interrupted your meal?"

"Yes, I am," answered the creature, with no sense of irony. "Might I finish it?"

"What? Are you kidding me?"

"I am not Kiddingme. I am Kreeble." She curtseyed toward him. "And I would like to continue feasting on your grits. Neither I nor my three companions had a chance to sample your ear grits before you ended our meal so abruptly."

"Sample this." Zenith threw his other shoe at her. Kreeble leapt backward as the projectile landed just short of its target.

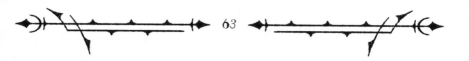

Kreeble bent her head over the shoe and sniffed. "No, thank you. The aroma is wonderful, but there are no grits in there." She brought both shoes back and held them out to Zenith, who snatched them and scooted away. He put his wet socks and shoes on, never letting his eyes stray from the bold little creature.

Kreeble's deep-set eyes returned his gaze. The gargoyle was only slightly larger than a squirrel, but top heavy. Blunt spikes ran along the top of her oversize head and down the back of her scale-covered body. Her arms were longer than her legs, and while her feet resembled cat's paws, her hands had five delicate fingers. She used one to stroke her jutting chin, like a chess player contemplating a gambit.

"Perhaps a trade," she ventured. "Is there anything I might offer you in exchange for your ear grits?"

Zenith walked away without answering.

He found Apogee's backpack. The dream image of her yelling at him flashed briefly across his mind. He wished it were just a figment of his imagination. When Zenith had hit his head and plunged through the ice, his body *and* his mind had been swallowed by the cold, indifferent darkness of the pond. His

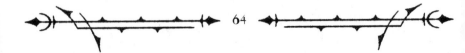

body had been pulled out quickly. It had taken most of his memories a little longer to resurface. Parts of that day were still a bit foggy, but the sound of his sister rooting against him was one thing he'd never forgotten.

He disrupted this pointless train of thought by checking the useless stuff inside the backpack. He pulled Apogee's textbook out. It was mostly dry. And heavy. He considered chucking it. Then he spotted Apogee's name written on the inside cover. Her comically bad penmanship almost made him laugh. He always had such a hard time deciphering anything she wrote. The chuckle died in his throat. Would he ever get the chance to struggle over a note from his sister again?

He put the book back in the bag after checking the rest of its paltry contents. Luckily, nothing was water damaged. Like Zenith, it was wet on the outside, but the inside was intact. He marveled at the fact that he was okay, considering all that'd happened yesterday. The abduction of Apogee, the attacks by Whichway Woods, the confrontation with the patchwork man, the second abduction of Apogee. And topping it all off, his ride in the raging rapids. He'd been knocked

unconscious, but the stream had apparently spat him back out and dumb luck had kept him otherwise unharmed. "I'll need a *lot* more dumb luck if I'm going to find Apogee," he muttered, and stood up.

"What? What is it you need?" Kreeble trotted toward him. "Are you hungry? I can show you the finest fungus in the forest. Or perhaps you would prefer to start your day with some nettles and bark."

"No, thank you." Zenith walked away from the creature. "I'm looking for my sister, not breakfast."

"Do you mean the other creature like yourself? You will not find her in Whichway Woods."

Zenith stopped and turned. "What do you know about Apogee?"

"Is that her name? If so, then I know two things. One, that her name is Apogee, and two, that she cannot be found inside this forest."

"Can you show me where she is?"

"No. But I can lead you the same way she was taken. If . . ." The gargoyle coyly turned away from Zenith. "If you make your ears available for my dining pleasure."

Zenith scoffed at the little creature. "Are you serious?"

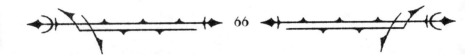

Kreeble examined herself with great earnestness. "I am not laughing nor crying. So, yes, I suppose you could call my current emotion 'serious.' Do you accept my offer? I will show you the way your sister traveled out of Whichway Woods in exchange for . . ." She screwed up her eyes shrewdly. "A five-minute feast of your ear grits."

Before Zenith could reply, there was a sudden rustling nearby as the giant rag doll came bursting out of the bushes and blocked their path. Zenith fell backward on his butt, then scrambled to get back up and away from the lumbering giant. The raggedy man uttered strangled noises as he had the night before.

"Good morning, Albert," said Kreeble, unperturbed. She curtsied toward the rag man. "Where are your scissors?"

Zenith watched in disbelief as the colossal doll stopped mid-stride, bowed formally to the gargoyle, and spoke to her in more muffled tones.

After listening for a moment, Kreeble sighed with frustration. "Hold on, Albert. This will never do."

The gargoyle scurried over to the giant's feet and then scampered up his tremendous legs and torso.

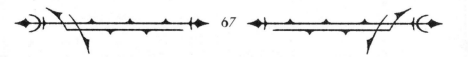

Kreeble stopped at his shoulder, and Albert bent his chin forward like a dog looking to be scratched. The gargoyle raised one long-fingered hand. Sharp claws extended from her fingers' blunt tips, and she used one to deftly cut the thread on the doll's buttoned-up mouth. One, two, three, four. The buttons all fell into Albert's waiting hand.

With his mouth undone, Albert spoke in a much calmer manner, but the noises he made were still incomprehensible to Zenith. "Ohiw pb vflvvruv dw krph. Glgq'w wklqn L'g qhhg wkhp."

"Left his scissors at home," Kreeble explained. "Did not think he would need them." The giant spoke again to the gargoyle perched on his shoulder. "Says there is usually no one to talk to in Whichway Woods."

Kreeble flushed. "Wait. What about me? What about Kribble, Krobble, and Krone?" Albert looked the other way and muttered. "We are *not* always too busy eating! You are being very insulting, Albert. My current emotion is now anger." Kreeble turned away from Albert's head and crossed her arms. The rag man whispered something more, and the gargoyle

perked up immediately. "Albert is inviting us to his home for breakfast!"

Zenith was suspicious. "Why do I have this feeling that *I'll* be the main course?"

Kreeble tilted her head quizzically. "I do not know. Do you often get this sort of feeling? Are you considered particularly tasty where you come from?"

Albert spoke before Zenith could, and Kreeble translated for him. "Albert says it was never his intention to scare you last night and offers this meal by way of apology. He says that he has no interest in eating you, no matter how flavorful you may be. He does not eat any sort of meat."

"Tell that to the turkey," Zenith said, and nodded toward the carcass that was poking out of the sack Raggedy Albert was carrying.

Kreeble looked confused again. "I cannot tell that bird anything. It is clearly dead." She turned toward Zenith and looked at him as if he might be crazy. "You can see that it is dead, can you not?"

Albert spoke once more. "Albert offers the flesh of the bird to you if that is what your kind likes to eat." The giant looked at his own body and said

something else. Kreeble scampered down to the rag doll's stomach and sliced off one of his belly buttons. Sawdust poured out for a few seconds before Kreeble pulled the gap closed. "This is what Albert puts in his body. He can eat nothing else."

"Fine. But what about my sister?"

"Albert cannot eat her either."

"I mean I need to find her as soon as possible."

"I can point you in the right direction, but GrahBhag is a large place," Kreeble said. "Are you sure you want to start your search on an empty stomach?"

Zenith thought for a moment. He was desperate to find his sister, but he was also starving, and the only "food" he had was a half-empty pack of gum. How was that going to sustain him long enough to rescue Apogee? Would he be able to discover something edible on his own? Could he really afford to turn down this invitation?

While these thoughts ran through his head, Zenith watched the rag man take a thread and needle from a small pouch. He swiftly sewed the button back onto his own belly while Kreeble held it closed. When he was done, Albert raised the needle to his

mouth and began to sew one of his mouth buttons back on, but Kreeble stopped him with a soft pat on his stomach and a small shake of her head.

The gentleness the two creatures displayed with each other, and the emptiness of his own stomach swayed Zenith. He asked Kreeble, "You're sure he just wants to dine together? I can eat all I want? No strings attached?"

"Do you want strings? Albert has plenty of thread, but I do not find it appetizing." The rag man interrupted her before she went on. "Albert says that you can eat till you are stuffed."

Zenith's stomach rumbled at the idea of being full. "Then I accept Albert's kind offer." Zenith bowed toward the giant. Albert returned the bow. Kreeble scrambled down the doll's leg, ran over, and began to climb up Zenith. He shook her off his ankle. "What are you doing?"

Kreeble looked up at him shrewdly. "I am taking my payment. It is all agreed. Albert and I will lead you out of Whichway Woods to his home. In return, I will feast on your ear grits as we travel." Zenith was speechless. "I will also act as translator at no additional charge." Then in a colder voice, she added,

"Or you may continue to wander alone, and we will have breakfast without you."

Zenith stayed silent, but slid his foot toward the gargoyle. Kreeble scrambled up his body and perched on his shoulder. He could feel her hot breath on his ear as she licked her lips. "Oh, this looks scrumptious!"

Mealtime

RAGGEDY **ALBERT LED** them through Whichway Woods quickly and with little difficulty. Occasionally a branch would grab at them, but Albert would break it before it could reach Zenith, who walked as closely behind the giant as was practical. His newfound sense of safety was shaken only once, when he heard the nearby footsteps of one of the unseen somethings from the night before. Albert noticed the noise and stopped to listen. The concealed creature quickly retreated.

Unfortunately, Kreeble was a much more persistent creature. She stayed firmly attached to Zenith's shoulder and "feasted" for the entire length of their trip through the forest. Thankfully, she kept her claws retracted and never scratched him. Her running commentary was what really grated on him, but there were useful warnings interspersed

throughout. "Oh yes, delightful!" *Slurp!* "Oh, this bit looks tasty!" *Nom nom*— "NO! Do not step there. That one is a tricking stone." *Nom nom nom.*

She finished cleaning out his left ear at the same time they emerged from the forest. Albert gestured at a small, isolated cottage just fifty feet outside the tree line.

"That is Albert's home. We are almost there. I shall have to hurry up and start on your right ear!" She clambered around Zenith's neck to his other shoulder.

He plucked her up and put her on the ground before she could dig in. "I think I've 'paid' enough for your services as guide."

Kreeble was very upset. "But right ear grits are the most succulent," she pleaded. "That is why I saved that ear for last!"

Zenith walked away. "Sorry. You snooze, you lose."

"I have not fallen asleep! How could I be asleep and still run after you? Please, just one taste!"

Albert's house was a humble log cabin, with a large number of unused logs strewn about the outside. It looked like the home of a disorganized but

very enthusiastic lumberjack. The smell of sawdust wafted toward Zenith as Albert opened the door and beckoned him inside. The décor was rather sparse. The only thing hanging on the walls was a crude, hand-carved clock with acorns for weights and twigs for clock hands. At first glance, the time appeared to be 8:15, but upon closer inspection, Zenith saw that the clockface was divided into nine hours rather than twelve. The roughly sculpted log furniture didn't look particularly comfortable. Zenith supposed that the giant rag doll was soft enough on his own and wouldn't need any extra padding wherever he chose to flop down.

Zenith chose to flop down in a large chair at a small dining table. Before him was an array of nuts and berries, only some of which he recognized. Albert gestured for him to eat. He was very hungry but still suspicious. "Why was all this food already prepared and waiting? How did you know you'd have guests?"

The rag doll muttered in his puzzling tongue.

"Albert is always making new friends, so he likes to have something waiting for them."

The giant muttered something more, lifted the

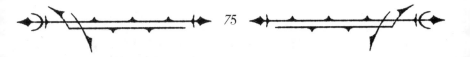

sack with the game bird inside, and disappeared down a dark hallway.

"He is going to prepare the bird for you, but it will take a while to cook, and he invites you to start eating what is already before you."

Zenith picked up what looked like a blackberry and gave it a cautious sniff. It smelled like a blackberry. He gave it a nibble. It tasted like a blackberry. And like heaven. He popped the whole thing into his mouth. The gush of sweet, tart juice overwhelmed him. For a moment, he thought he might faint. Instead, he dug into the pile of nuts and berries with both hands, unable to gobble them fast enough to satisfy his newly awakened hunger.

Raggedy Albert came back into the room, carrying three logs. He came to Zenith's side of the table, placed the logs on the ground, and gestured for the boy to stand up. He did so, but stayed close to the table and continued to shovel food into his mouth.

Albert set the first log on its end next to Zenith and studied it for a moment before discarding it. He did the same with the other two and, after a thoughtful pause, brought the first one back. He rotated it slightly and then looked between it and Zenith.

Having made up his mind, Albert took the chosen log and placed it on a nearby pedestal, which was really just another log.

As Zenith returned to his seat and continued eating, the giant rag doll used a small hand ax to remove the bark from the stump. When Albert was done, he gathered up the pieces of bark and placed them on the far side of the table, away from Zenith's diminishing cache of food. Kreeble scrambled up onto the table and sorted through the bark. She quickly found a foul-looking, disease-ridden piece and began to munch on it contentedly. Zenith hadn't noticed the gargoyle's absence from the dining table. He hadn't been very quick noticing Albert's ax either. His stomach had been in control since that first blackberry. But now his brain was coming back from its brief break.

Zenith paused his eating and looked at his two companions. Kreeble was still gnawing on her first piece of bark, but her eyes were already roaming over the pile in front of her. Albert had put down his ax and was working at the log with a small hammer and chisel. "So, what can you tell me about the creature that captured my sister?"

Both beings stopped what they were doing, but neither looked at him. Zenith went on. "Albert, you must've seen the thing that pulled her into the river last night."

The rag man did not respond. Instead, he bent closer to the log and went back to work with his tools.

Zenith turned to the gargoyle. "Kreeble, you told me she was taken out of Whichway Woods. But by what?"

Kreeble very deliberately lifted the chunk of bark she was eating so it hid her eyes from his gaze.

Zenith impatiently batted it down and continued. "What is that weird hairball-spider thing, and what does it want with my—"

"It is a child of the Wurm, and no one dares to question its actions," Kreeble blurted.

"What? What does that mean? A child of the *what*?"

A kitchen timer began sounding in another room, and Albert hastily left to attend to it. Kreeble whispered at him harshly, "We do not speak of the Great Wurm or its minions or its children with such disrespect!" She sat back. "You are being rude."

Zenith was baffled by this critique of his etiquette. Before he could recover, Albert returned carrying

a large platter filled with what looked vaguely like roast turkey. Very vaguely. Parts of the bird were randomly strewn around the plate as if the poor beast had been torn apart before being cooked. The skin was entirely absent. Instead, chunks of meat were intermingled with pulpy bits that could only be the bird's internal organs. Zenith thought it looked less like Thanksgiving dinner and more like a grisly, gristly crime scene.

And yet the aroma still made his mouth water and his stomach rumble. He reached over what looked like the heart and grabbed a leg. The bird was a little overcooked and a bit dry, but Zenith couldn't afford to be picky. Asking about Shlurp and this "Great Wurm" character had offended his two companions and probably lost him any chance of further help. If he was going to save his sister on his own, he would need all the energy he could muster. He would "eat till he was stuffed," as Albert had apparently put it. Eat everything put in front of him. Except for the troubling turkey guts.

They ate in silence. Zenith gradually consumed the bird one disturbing piece at a time, while Kreeble worked her way through the diseased tree bark. All

the while, Albert chiseled away at his block of wood.

When nothing was left but a hodgepodge of re-pulsive blobs that he just couldn't stomach, Zenith pushed his chair back from the table and got up. "I want to thank you both for a fine meal." The formal tone of his own voice took him by surprise. Perhaps Kreeble was wearing off on him. He fumbled through the rest. "But I must now leave and . . . because . . . I, uh, have to get going and find my sister."

The giant gestured for him to sit back down and muttered something urgently.

"Albert objects to your leaving. He says that he has not made you into his friend yet."

At that, the rag man rushed out of the room in a bit of a panic.

Zenith picked up the backpack from the floor. "Tell him that I am very thankful for the meal and feel closer to him than I do to any other living rag doll I've ever met."

Albert rushed back in carrying a tarnished silver tray with a porcelain teapot, a cracked teacup, and a plate of sugar cookies. He put himself between Zenith and the door. "Albert insists that you must have some tea if you are to become his friend," Kreeble said.

With a frustrated sigh, Zenith resumed his place at the table while the giant served him tea. He tossed an entire cookie into his mouth, then raised his teacup toward Albert in a half-hearted toast before taking a gulp. It was lukewarm and sour. Nevertheless, he drained the cup quickly to make sure his hulking host was satisfied.

He put the cup down with a clatter. "There. Now we are friends." He got up from his chair and grabbed the backpack once more. He offered his hand to Raggedy Albert, hoping that a firm handshake would persuade the giant to step aside and let him be on his way. Albert did not raise his hand in response. He just stared at Zenith's hand. He stared at it so intensely that Zenith began to wonder if there was something wrong with it.

Zenith looked at his own hand. There *was* something wrong with it. It was fuzzy. No. Not fuzzy. Out of focus. *Wait*, he thought fuzzily. *Is that my hand's fault, or should I blame my eyes? Are* they *the fuzzy ones, or is it my whole head?*

His fuzzy-feeling feet gave out on him, and Zenith fell forward into Albert's waiting arms.

Making Friends

ZENITH COULDN'T MOVE his arms, and kicking his feet did no good. He was suspended in midair, his body wrapped tightly in string. Kevin Churl held him up off the ground by the end of the string. Kevin was eight feet tall, with button eyes and a button mouth, and was dunking him repeatedly into a giant teacup out on the frozen pond in Kalikov Park. Zenith's feet shot through with pain each time his skates hit the bottom of the cup. The tea inside burned his legs. Kevin was laughing. All Zenith's friends were laughing. Even Apogee was laughing. Apogee laughed and writhed on her belly and skittered across the ice on nine black, spindly legs. Kevin lifted Zenith twice as high as before and then dropped him. His skates shattered the bottom of the cup and the ice below it, and Zenith plunged into the murky depths of the freezing water.

Zenith awoke with a gasp. The dream was over, but he still couldn't move his arms or legs. He was wrapped from ankle to shoulder in golden yellow yarn. The festive color failed to amuse Zenith. He was even less pleased when he looked around the dark, unfamiliar room.

He was surrounded by a menagerie of bizarre beasts. They gawked at him with button eyes. Their mouths were agape as if to roar or scream, but the room was silent; their ability to make any sort of noise was at an end. Their bodies were held together by haphazard seams and random clusters of buttons, as if an impatient child with a penchant for doll making had been trained in taxidermy.

Somewhere behind him came the clatter of wooden blinds opening, and the dim room was flooded with slatted light. Albert walked past him and over to a large worktable in the center of the room. A rough-hewn wood figure resembling the turkey bird stood on the table behind a large pile of salt. There were also a variety of ominous-looking tools.

Zenith tore his eyes away from them with some effort and gazed into the solemn face of the rag man.

"Look, Albert," he began shakily. "I'm sorry if I've offended you."

Albert plunged his hand into the pile of salt, pulled out the desiccated skin of the turkey bird, and held it up in front of his button eyes. The skin retained the bird's plumage, but its feathers didn't obscure the long slit that ran from its belly to its beak.

"I'm happy to hang out for a little while longer if that will . . . solidify our friendship." Zenith tried to sound hopeful but failed.

Albert took the skin and slowly fitted it over the wooden carving of the bird. The delicacy and care he took easing the skin over the wood reminded Zenith of a tailor dressing an esteemed client.

"Okay, great. So, we'll hang out for a little while and then you'll untie me, and I'll get going."

Albert made no acknowledgment. Instead, the giant finished adjusting the skin and swiftly stitched the seam. He then reached into his pouch and pulled out a handful of buttons. He placed all but one onto the table, then adorned the seam with the small blue button he'd selected. After a minute he retrieved another button from the table and then a third. He moved quickly and skillfully. Albert paused and took

a step back to assess things. The skin fit snugly over its new wooden frame, but there was still a little slack in the sewn-up stomach. After popping a stitch to create a small gap in the seam, Albert flipped the taxidermy bird upside down and brought the belly close to his face.

It looked like Albert was going to kiss his creation. Instead, a grotesque gurgling noise escaped the rag doll's throat as he regurgitated sawdust into the gap in the belly seam. Like a mama bird feeding its young, Albert fed his creation till its tummy was full.

Albert sewed the belly completely shut, decorated it with another shiny button, and placed the finished piece back on the table. He leaned away from it, admiring his own handiwork. And then, for the first time since Zenith had woken up, Albert turned toward the boy he had tied up in the corner.

Zenith suddenly wanted nothing more than for Albert to go back to ignoring him. Instead, the giant held his gaze as he reached down behind his worktable and brought out a new carving. Zenith's mouth went dry. He blinked his eyes several times to confirm, or perhaps deny, what he was seeing. The figure

was of Zenith himself. It was life-size and posed with its arm outstretched, as if it were searching for something. Or warding something off.

Albert whispered and pointed at the boy. Zenith didn't want to know what he was saying.

"Now it is time for you to become Albert's friend."

Zenith looked to his right and saw Kreeble sitting in the lap of one of the stuffed beasts. The animal looked like a cross between a raccoon and a small bear. It was sitting on its haunches and posed as if it was about to eat the pine cone it held in its claws. The gargoyle unconsciously copied the pose as she munched on another piece of tree bark.

"Friend?" Zenith said, his voice low and ragged. "Is that your idea of a joke?"

"No. That is not a joke. Here is a joke: What is always full *and* always empty but never . . . Wait, no, that is more of a riddle."

"You knew he had this planned all along. And you just helped him lure me here. And for what? Some tree bark?"

Kreeble raised her eyebrows. "You knew he had this planned as well. I told you what he had planned. He said you could eat till you were stuffed. You

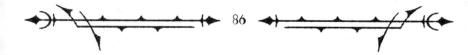

have eaten, and now you will be stuffed. This is how Albert makes all his friends. Do you not see?" She waved her arms at the room's occupants and took another bite of bark.

Albert said something in his garbled, strange language and came toward Zenith. The boy fought to break free, but stopped when the giant went past. He could hear a door open and close behind him.

"Albert apologizes. You were not meant to wake up before you became his friend, but he measured the dose incorrectly. He is going to make another batch of Lethar Tea. This pot will be much stronger."

Zenith struggled again, but it was no use. His bonds were not only festively colored, but also diabolically secure. He had a dreadful moment as he pictured his taxidermy self: his mouth frozen in a wide blue-button smile and his stomach sewn shut with the golden yarn.

He closed his eyes and shook his head to banish the image. When he opened them again, he was looking at Kreeble. The gargoyle was scraping the fungus from a fresh piece of tree bark with the claw on her forefinger.

"Kreeble! Come over here," whispered Zenith.

"Come over here and set me free. You can slice through this yarn with your claws."

The gargoyle looked at him doubtfully. "Yes, I *can* slice through that yarn, but why would I *want* to? Albert would be very cross with me if I interfered."

"Are you really going to let your friend kill me?"

"F-friend?!" sputtered Kreeble. "I would never be Albert's friend. Look what he does to his friends!" She took in the whole room with another expansive wave. Then she turned slyly to Zenith. "So, I ask you again, *why* would I want to free you?"

Ah. The gargoyle wasn't rejecting the idea, she was negotiating the terms. "I'll, uh," stammered Zenith. "I'll let you eat the grits out of my right ear!"

The creature's eyes lit up. This was obviously what she wanted to hear. But she quickly realized she'd given herself away and tried to appear less interested. "Sounds intriguing. And how long would I get to feast?"

"Uh, I don't know. I mean, how long do you need?" Zenith asked anxiously. "Can't you eat it pretty quickly? Take as long as you need to eat it all."

"*All* of your ear grits! You are offering me all the grits your ears will ever produce? I accept!" Kreeble

quickly ran over and set to work on the yarn around Zenith's legs.

"What? No, that's not what I meant. I meant whatever was in my ear right now. I'm not giving you a lifetime supply of my earwax!"

Kreeble dropped the strand of yarn she was about to cut through. "Well then, I do not think you have much lifetime left."

The kitchen timer sounded from the other room, followed by the clatter of dishes. His tea was ready, and his time was up. "Fine!" He exhaled sharply. "You've got an all-access pass to my ears! Just cut me loose, and let's get out of here!"

Kreeble sliced through the yarn in three places. Zenith stood up, and his bonds fell to the floor. He took a quick look around the taxidermy room. There were several small windows, but only one door. The only way out was the same way Albert was about to come in. And he could hear the giant approaching.

A moment later, Albert came through the door carrying the silver tray with the teapot and cup; no cookies this time. He stopped suddenly when he saw the yarn on the floor. The rag doll calmly walked to the center of the room and placed the tea service

on his worktable. He grabbed a threaded needle and some buttons off the surface. Albert spoke loudly to his room full of friends. "L nqrz brx'uh vwloo khuh!"

Zenith and Kreeble crouched behind one of the largest taxidermy beasts as the gargoyle whispered, "He says that he knows you are still here." Zenith shushed her, but she kept translating. "He does not understand why you are turning down his friendship. None of the others have ever done so. He promises you a 'pleasant journey,' but I think he means a painless death."

Zenith covered the gargoyle's mouth with one hand and scooped her up off the ground. Albert stood by his worktable, making repetitive motions around the back of his head with his floppy hands and continuing his speech to the assembled audience. The crowd of taxidermy friends was so dense that Zenith was able to sneak around the outside of the circle of beasts without attracting Albert's attention. And as he crept slowly toward the door, Zenith moved out of the giant's line of sight.

Zenith reached the end of the taxidermy menagerie, but there were still fifteen feet of open ground between his last hiding place and the door. Luckily,

he'd traveled about halfway around the circle, and Albert was now facing away from him. As long as the patchwork behemoth didn't turn around, Zenith could move quietly toward the exit without being seen. He took a moment and stilled his breathing. He gave Kreeble a meaningful look and tightened his grip over her mouth. He slowly stepped out into the open.

Just then, Albert ceased his repetitive movement and dropped his hands, revealing two new button eyes sewn onto the back of his head. One eye dangled loosely from a length of scarlet thread, but the other was secured tightly in place.

And it clearly saw Zenith.

The rag doll's legs trembled, and then, one after the other, the creature thrust them backward till they bent the wrong way round. There was no sickening crack as Albert's knees were broken. He had no knees to break. He raised his arms backward and ran at the boy without having to turn around.

Zenith tucked Kreeble under one arm like a football, grabbed a taxidermy deer-thing, and pulled it down in front of Albert before running out of the room. He heard a cry of alarm from behind him, but

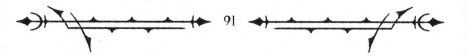

Zenith didn't take the time to look back. If he was going to outrun the long-legged creature, he needed to move as fast as he possibly could.

He sprinted through the dark hall, through the front room, and out the front door. He ran down the short path away from the cabin. He ran away from the nearby forest. He pumped his legs so fast that he threw himself off-balance and fell forward, dropping Kreeble and landing elbows first. He scrambled back to his feet as quickly as he could, expecting it wouldn't be fast enough. But when he looked back, he saw he wasn't being pursued.

Raggedy Albert stood in the doorway of the distant cabin, holding the taxidermy deer-thing under one arm and shaking his fist at Zenith. He was yelling at them in his cryptic language.

Kreeble sighed. "I suppose that is the last time I will ever have breakfast with Albert."

Getting Away

IF KREEBLE WAS upset over the loss of breakfast privileges at Albert's house, she soon recovered. She set up shop on Zenith's shoulder and dug into his right ear. After a few minutes of munching, Zenith heard her admonishing herself. "Now, slow yourself, Kreeble. Savor this fine feast. No need to rush. Ooh, but I must have that bit right away!"

While Kreeble busied herself with his ear, Zenith put one foot in front of the other as quickly as he could. As they got farther from the forest, the mossy ground cover receded. The scales and hide of the horrible bag were once again visible below his feet. The stitched seam in the ground also reappeared. This change of terrain felt like progress. He was certainly happy to get away from Whichway Woods and Raggedy Albert. But he needed to do more than just get *away*. He needed to get *to* his

sister. He had no idea how to do that. He had no idea where to go.

So he stopped.

"Kreeble," he said as he turned his head and leaned left, trying to get a look at the creature on his shoulder. "Where should I go? Is there some nearby town where my sister might've been taken, or where someone can tell me what's happened to her?"

"Please face forward," sighed the exasperated gargoyle. "You are making it difficult for me to eat."

"Please answer my question, and then you can eat."

"I will answer your question *while* I eat, thank you very much," said the stubborn little beast. Zenith turned his head. "Ahh, much better." He felt her finger scoop up some earwax, and then, with a full mouth, she replied. "No."

"What?" Zenith leaned and looked again. The gargoyle put a finger to his chin and patiently turned his head forward again.

"There is nowhere to go. There is no one to speak to. Because there is no one in GrahBhag that dares to question the will of the Holey Wurm or its minions."

"What is this worm thing you keep talking about?"

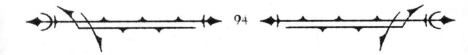

The gargoyle glanced around nervously and spoke more loudly than necessary. "I do not *talk* of the Great Wurm! I sing Its praises! I praise Its being! All hail the Great and Holey Wurm!" She turned back to his ear and whispered into it. "The Wurm rules all. If its child has taken your sister, the Wurm has want of her. It would be best to abandon your quest."

"But you said you would help me save Apogee."

"Find her, not save her," Kreeble corrected him. "I agreed to point you in the right direction." The gargoyle waved at the path before them without looking away from his ear. "That is the right direction. But if you intend to defy the Great Wurm, you will be on your own."

Zenith opened his mouth, then snapped it shut. He stubbornly trudged forward again. He had never liked hearing "no" and made a point of pursuing things others considered to be foolhardy. He'd ridden his ten-speed on the half-pipe at the local skate park, attempted to tame a couple of feral cats with a can of tuna, and tried to drink a two-liter bottle of pop in under two minutes on a dare. His bike had been totaled, his arms had been covered in scratches,

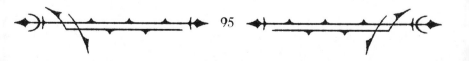

and most of the soda had gone down his shirt instead of his throat, but no permanent damage had been done. The stakes here were a lot higher, the danger more palpable, but Zenith was determined to press on. He *would* find help, and he *would* save his sister. He had no other choice.

The stitches they'd been following took a sharp turn to the left, and for lack of a better idea, Zenith, with Kreeble in tow, did the same. Around this bend, the terrain transitioned as the hide and scales they'd been treading upon gave way to a dirt road. The stitches remained visible, however, and ran into the distance, down the road's center. Zenith spotted a small band of travelers approaching on foot from the opposite direction.

Their manner of dress was recognizable enough, if a little outdated, and for a moment he thought the group was human. His spirits lifted at the sight of them, although as they drew nearer, he grew unsettled by the shape of them. They were decidedly *not* human. Their bodies were boxy, as broad from front to back as they were from side to side. Their hands were twice as wide as his own and sported three plump fingers and a stubby thumb. Bare feet, visible

below their trousers and skirts, were also immense, but each calloused foot ended in twelve tiny toes. Zenith broke into a cold sweat as the creatures came closer and their sallow-skinned faces turned his way. Their wide-set eyes were bloodshot, their noses bulbous. Their jagged teeth were dark yellow in color and fearsome in appearance.

Zenith braced for an attack.

Instead, the largest of them merely nodded at him and said, "G'day to ye, yoong stranger," as they passed him by. The accent was heavy, and the courteous demeanor unexpected. It took a moment for Zenith to catch up. He turned toward the receding group, his mouth slightly agape.

The smallest of the travelers looked back at him and laughed. "Look't, Mamsie. Deh aufwelter is all sixxy-sevens!"

The one that must have been its mother gave the child a gentle tap on his shoulder. "Don't be rude, Gregor!" She opened her mouth into what Zenith supposed was a smile, though the helter-skelter arrangement of her teeth made it hard to be certain. "Pardon my aufspring, yoong sir."

"No, no problem," mumbled Zenith.

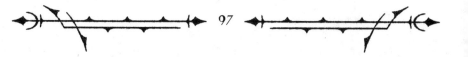

They'd all stopped and were looking back at him. One muttered to another, "Sooch a thick accent."

The large leader made to leave and repeated, "G'day to ye."

But Mamsie stood still. "Is there somethin' ye need, yoong sir?" She glanced at Kreeble. "Is that creecher on yer shoulder botherin' ye? Be it pet or pest?"

The gargoyle hopped off Zenith's shoulder and landed in front of him. "I will have you know I am an invited guest!"

"I'm wondering," ventured Zenith, "if you've seen my sister?"

"Is she a funny-looking aufwelter like ye?" asked Gregor. He began to laugh, but Mamsie put a stop to that with a stern look.

"Yes, she looks like me. She was kidnapped by this horrible hairball-spider thing." He glanced down at Kreeble. "I think you'd call it a 'child of the Wurm.'"

Dead silence. Then a nervous murmur ran through the group as they shrank away from Zenith.

"What did ye just say?" Mamsie asked in a whisper.

"He took the name of Its Allfullness in vain!" cried a frightened Gregor.

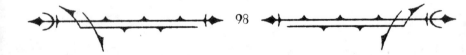

"He'll bring the wrath of Its Noneness down on us all!" boomed the voice of the leader.

Zenith raised his hand as if to calm them all down. "I'm not trying to get anyone in trouble. I just want my sister back. I'm happy to leave this stupid Wurm thing alone if I can—"

A cry of anguish arose from the crowd. They averted their eyes and hurried away from him.

All except for an old woman. She lurched toward Zenith and placed her thick three-fingered hand on his shoulder. Her face was concealed by a dark head-scarf except for one exposed, tearstained eye. "Turn back," she rasped. "Return from whence ye came. 'Tis folly to challenge the Great and Holey Wurm. Those that dare, pay an awful price."

The old woman pulled back her scarf, and Zenith recoiled. What was revealed was less of a face and more an angry scar of ruined flesh. Her other eye was melted shut, as was half of her mouth. There were cryptic symbols burned into her cheek and running across her hairless scalp, as if she'd been branded. "This. This is what awaits those that provoke Its Allfullness the Wurm." She slowly backed away from Zenith without dropping her gaze. "Turn back."

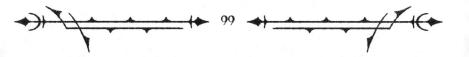

Turning Back

ZENITH STOOD ALONE in the middle of the road. The old woman's warning echoed in his head. The image of her scarred face filled his mind.

A sudden tug on his pant leg brought Zenith back to himself. Kreeble said, "If I may," and then crawled back up to his shoulder without waiting for a reply. The gargoyle scooped some grits from his right ear. "All this excitement has made me quite hungry." She began munching contentedly.

"Is there anything that doesn't make you hungry?" Zenith asked bitterly. He quickly added, "Don't answer that."

"As you say, I will not answer that, for it is a question that makes no sense. Much like your absurd quest to save your sister."

"So, no one will help me?"

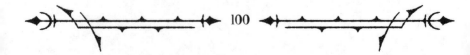

"You saw for yourself how others react when you mention the Great and Holey Wurm."

He had seen it. What the gargoyle said was true. And yet it wasn't really an answer to his question. He tried again. "There's no one, absolutely no one, who will help or tell me anything useful?"

"Until just now, I have never met anyone who has dared oppose the Wurm. And you saw what happened to her." She gestured toward the retreating travelers without taking her eyes off his ear. "Now please be quiet. You are interrupting my meal." She scooped another finger's worth of wax into her mouth.

Again, this wasn't really an answer. For a creature who usually spoke so literally, the gargoyle was being vague and evasive.

"You're saying that there's no one who will tell me anything?"

"I am saying nothing. I am trying to eat."

"I have no chance of saving her from whatever Shlurp or this Wurm has planned for her?"

"The Holey Wurm rules all. And all obey Its Allfullness. All serve Its Noneness."

Zenith turned on his heel and took an exaggerated step back the way they'd just come. "Well then,"

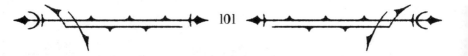

he said as he plucked Kreeble off his shoulder and put her down on the ground, "I might as well head home." He straightened up, gave out a loud sigh, and walked back toward the woods.

"Wait, what is happening?" asked the gargoyle. "Why have you interrupted my meal? Where are you going without Kreeble?"

"If I can't save my sister, then I have no business in GrahBhag. I'm going back to my own world. And you would *not* be welcome there. Consider your all-access pass to my ear grits revoked." He raised his arm over his head, waved goodbye, and quickened his pace.

"No!" He could hear the pain in Kreeble's voice. She made some small fretting noises as she ran after him. "Please wait!"

Zenith slowed down but didn't stop. He didn't look back. "Wait for what? You said no one will help me. No one's going to defy the Wurm. So how can I find my sister?"

Kreeble grunted. "All right, all right. There might be one way to find her."

Zenith stopped and turned around. He was careful not to smile. Instead, he crossed his arms and

looked down at the gargoyle suspiciously. "Tell me how."

"I will do better." Kreeble's mood brightened instantly. "I will *show* you how." She headed toward Zenith's leg, but he stepped back and put a hand over each ear.

"Show me *first*."

The Scribe

KREEBLE LED HIM the same way they'd been heading before Zenith had pretended to leave. The gargoyle hopped back and forth over the stitches in the ground as she went. She stopped every few minutes to turn around and glower at Zenith, making sure he understood how unhappy she was about having her meal interrupted.

Zenith said in an amused voice, "I've never seen someone who was so mad still manage to skip so happily down the road. Why are you hopping over the stitches?"

Kreeble lifted her nose and looked away as she replied. "In GrahBhag, we have a saying. 'To keep free of trouble and hitches, mind your path and follow the stitches.'"

Zenith replied, "In my world we say, 'Step on a crack, break your mother's back. Step on a line,

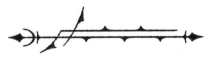 

break your father's spine.'"

The gargoyle looked horrified. "Why, in the name of the Wurm, would you do such violence to those who birthed you?"

Zenith didn't bother to explain. Kreeble's question was ridiculous, but his parents *were* suffering right now. Both of their kids had mysteriously disappeared, and it was all his fault. He started scratching at his scar.

Kreeble noticed this nervous gesture. "Did someone step on something and injure *you*?"

Zenith forced himself to stop scratching. "No. I hurt my head playing hockey."

The gargoyle looked confused. "I am not familiar with this word."

"Hockey is a sport. A game. I've liked hitting and kicking things since I was a baby, so my parents pointed me away from the living room furniture and toward sports at a pretty young age."

"And these things that you hit, they hit back?"

"No, the injury was my sister's fault, actually." Zenith scowled and looked down at his feet. "I was about to score the winning goal when Apogee cried out and distracted me. The guy I was playing against,

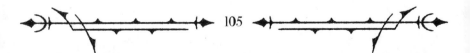

Kevin, caught up and tripped me, and I fell. And after that—"

Kreeble held up a hand to shush him. "We are here," she said, and then scurried forward alongside the stitches and up a small incline about fifty feet ahead. She stopped in front of a line of large rocks. They were shaped irregularly, but spaced at such precise intervals as to suggest deliberate placement. Zenith climbed up after the gargoyle. He stopped beside her and peered over the rock line.

The rocks formed a circle around a shallow valley. Twenty or more sets of stitches, each a different color, ran into the valley from various directions and converged at the circle's center under one colossal tree shimmering in the red light of the midday sun. "That is the Collectory of GrahBhag," whispered Kreeble. "And that is its Scribe." She pointed her finger toward the bottom of the tree.

A raven the size of a horse was hurriedly hopping back and forth below the branches of the majestic tree. "That giant bird knows where Apogee is?" asked Zenith.

"If any creature knows the fate of your sister and is willing to tell it, it will be the Scribe." Kreeble

clambered over the rocks. "Come. We must pay our respects and beseech the Scribe for his favor." Zenith stepped over the rocks and followed the gargoyle down the other side of the hill.

Kreeble kept her head bowed as they approached, and at first Zenith did the same. But he could feel the looming presence of the immense tree, and after a few moments, he raised his head to get a closer look at it. Zenith's feet faltered as he saw the Collectory clearly for the first time. What he'd mistaken for a tree was something much more extraordinary. The valley's multitude of brightly colored stitches converged to form its roots. They plunged into the ground through a circle of massive brass eyelets around the Collectory's base. The tree's trunk was composed of these selfsame stitches, which reemerged from the ground as a rainbow-colored cord, and a tower of enormous oak thimbles around which the cord was coiled. As this cord climbed ever higher, strands split off and radiated outward to create the structure's branches. The strands split again and again to form smaller branchlets, each of which held a chalkboard the size of a small school notebook and colored green, like his sneakers. Some of these

slates were blank, while others bore writing, but Zenith wasn't close enough to read what was written on them.

Zenith had the strong impression that the Collectory had sprung up naturally. No, not naturally. *Magically.* There was some otherworldly energy emanating from it. *Maybe that's because you are in some other world,* thought Zenith.

His reverie was interrupted by a low hiss. Zenith looked around and saw that he'd strayed away from Kreeble, who'd turned to the right and was now gesturing for him to follow. He jogged the short distance to the gargoyle, and they continued together around the perimeter of the Collectory toward the Scribe.

As they approached, the air took on the smell of a classroom. Zenith saw that the bird was moving pieces of chalk from one large pile to several smaller piles, sorting it by color. The raven was a bit larger than he'd originally thought, and better dressed as well. The black bird was wearing an emerald green sweater-vest and a large pair of gold-rimmed spectacles. His dapper attire contrasted with the state of his wings, which were riddled with holes.

Kreeble called out to the raven, "Greetings to

you, O Scribe of the Collectory of GrahBhag. We are humble seekers of the History and the Details and the Truth." Kreeble placed her left hand over her forehead, then her mouth, and finally her heart. "Please grant us the smallest moment of—"

"Yes, yes, greetings," the bird grumbled without looking up. "Tell me, do you see any iridescent chalk in here? Hugh has left everything in the most dreadful disorder, and I cannot find my special iridescent chalk."

Kreeble seemed puzzled by the interruption. "Uhhmm. We seek humbly for . . ."

"Yes, yes. You seek History and Details and such. I heard you the first time. But where is that blasted chalk?!"

Kreeble looked at Zenith helplessly. Zenith screwed up his face. Was she really looking for guidance from him? He took a step forward, reached toward the chalk pile, and said, "We're happy to help you loo—"

The enormous bird pecked at his hand, barely missing his forefinger. "Use your eyes, not your hands! None but the Scribe may wield the enchanted chalk!" After a moment of awkward silence, the

raven suddenly exclaimed, "Aha! There you are!" He plunged his beak down into the disordered pile and emerged with a long piece of sparkling chalk. Its color shifted from yellow to blue-green to purple as he raised it triumphantly. He chuckled as he hopped over and placed it on an ornately carved but weathered wooden rolltop desk, which stood by the sorted piles of chalk. The raven admired the iridescent chalk for a moment as it twinkled, then swiveled quickly to face them. "Now, what brings such unworthy creatures before the Great Scribe?" he squawked loudly.

Kreeble smiled at Zenith. She lowered her head again. "We are humble seekers of the History and the Details and the Truth. Please grant us the smallest moment of your time and the tiniest morsel of your vast knowledge."

"And what new knowledge can *you* offer the Scribe?" asked the haughty bird.

"Pardon me, honorable Scribe. We seek knowledge. We do not offer it."

"This," pronounced the raven with an expansive wave of his hole-ridden wings, "is the Collectory. The Scribe *collects* knowledge. He does not *dispense*

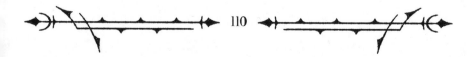

it." He looked back and forth between Zenith and Kreeble. "With those he finds worthy he may, on occasion, *exchange* knowledge. So, I ask again, what knowledge can you offer?"

"Knowledge, knowledge . . ." The gargoyle's eyes darted around nervously. They came to rest on Zenith's face, and she gestured dramatically at him. "My companion is a traveler from Terra Firmament. He has many Details of his home to share."

The Scribe seemed intrigued. He ogled Zenith through the lenses of his oversize glasses. His eyes looked huge and hungry. "Well, well, from Terra Firmament, you say. Rare to have a visitor from that troubled land." He resumed a more skeptical expression. "Rare, but not unheard of. Others of your kind have imparted the History and Details of your homeland. What have you to add?"

It was Zenith's turn to stammer. "Um. Uh . . . I can tell you the latest news and sports scores. 'Current events' I'd guess you'd call it." He swiveled the backpack off his shoulder. "And I've got this physics book if you want more intense scientific stuff."

"Science? Did you say you have a book about science?" The bird used its beak to pull open the

backpack's main pocket and gazed with wonder at the book inside. "This is a Firman craft that the Scribe has long sought the knowledge of."

"And you're welcome to it," said Zenith before he pulled the backpack away. "But in *exchange*, you'll tell me what you know about my sister." The blank look on the bird's face worried Zenith. "*Do* you know something about my sister? She's been taken from my world and brought to GrahBhag. If you don't know anythi—"

"The Collectory and its Scribe hold ALL History and Details of GrahBhag!" The indignant bird hopped over to the Collectory, snatched three of the lowest hanging chalkboard leaves with his beak, and hopped back. He dropped them onto the desk gently. "First, we will hear about your trip, then we must delve into this wondrous book of yours, and after that, we can discuss your sister." He spun around to a small pile of aqua blue chalk and snatched a piece off the top, then turned back to the desk and held the chalk in the tip of his beak over one of the blank chalkboards. He cleared his throat theatrically and spoke out of the side of his mouth in his most formal tone. "Creature of Terra Firmament! Speak the Details of your journey

so that the Scribe may increase the knowledge of the Collectory!"

"Well, my name is Zenith Maelstrom and—"

"Spell your name!" croaked the raven. Zenith spelled it, and the bird copied it onto the chalkboard in elegant handwriting. Or, in this case, *beak*writing. "Continue!" the bird intoned.

"Yes, well, I, uh, have a fourteen-year-old sister named Apogee. She's been brought here against her will. Look, if you could just tell me what you know . . ."

The raven wrote as Zenith spoke, and now the chalkboard read, "Zenith Maelstrom has a fourteen-year-old sister named Apogee."

Zenith was about to continue when a loud shriek split the air. The hairs on the back of his neck stood up. It sounded like a bird of prey about to attack.

The Seeker

THERE WAS A second loud shriek, but this one was clearly a cry of laughter. It ended with a loud shout of, "Muncie!" Zenith looked up to see a second humongous raven flying toward them very quickly. This second bird had a long, fluttering scarf around its neck, the same emerald green as the Scribe's vest. As he drew close, the second bird dove sharply toward the ground. The force behind his own landing seemed to surprise him, and he blundered toward them, waving his wings wildly.

Zenith and Kreeble backed away quickly. The Scribe scooped up his treasured iridescent chalk, then hopped out of the way as the other raven barreled into the chalk piles. The Scribe croaked angrily. "Hugh! I've just sorted those. Oh, if you weren't my brother, I'd have you before the Inquisitor on charges!"

The other raven brushed the multicolored chalk

dust off his feathers. "Sorry, Muncie, I'm just so excited. I've flown straight from the village of Threadbare with the most delicious Details. It seems that young Lorelei has finally had her babies. But instead of twins, she's had triplets, and the father is none too pleased—"

"Slow down and hold on. Slow down and hold on." The Scribe placed his special chalk back on the desk. "Let me find the proper color." He examined the batch of chalk strewn on the ground, sifting through it with one foot. "Lime green is the color for Threadbare. Oh, where is it?" He fluttered his wing at his brother while he continued to look. "Introduce yourself to our guests, Hugh. The soft, fleshy one is from Terra Firmament."

"A Firman, you say." Hugh half flew, half stumbled across the short distance to Zenith. "Well, it looks like I've been missing some very important Details right here at home!"

"Missing things and misplacing things. Missing things and misplacing things," muttered Muncie as he continued sifting through the chalk. His weary voice suggested this was an ongoing problem. Zenith could easily imagine Apogee adopting

the same tone when haranguing him about his own shortcomings.

Hugh ignored his brother's testiness and continued in his own upbeat manner. "A pleasure to meet you." He bowed his head. "I am the Seeker of GrahBhag, collector of knowledge. But everybody calls me Hugh." The bird lifted his head, tilted it at Zenith, and waited. "Don't be rude, Firman, introduce yourself!"

"Uh, my name is Zenith Maelstrom. Pleased to meet you. I'm trying to find my—"

"Aha! Knew it. Speaks Anglish. He's from Angleland." He gave Zenith an appraising look. "Or maybe Fireland . . ."

"Don't be dim," sighed Muncie. "Listen to his accent. He's clearly from Merry-Caw." The Scribe bent down and picked a lime green piece of chalk up off the ground. He turned to the desk, pushed Zenith's chalkboard aside, and held the chalk over one of the other two. He cleared his throat and spoke. "Seeker of GrahBhag! Speak the Details concerning Lorelei of Threadbare so that the Scribe may increase the knowledge of the Collectory!"

Hugh flew with enthusiasm over to his brother

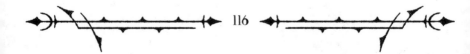

and slammed into the side of the desk. The desk was big and heavy and barely moved. Muncie didn't move at all. He seemed to be accustomed to his brother's clumsiness. Kreeble walked over to join them, and Zenith reluctantly followed. None of this was getting him any closer to finding Apogee.

"As you know, Lorelei has been overdue for a month now, and her husband, Yoseph, has been beside himself," began Hugh. "I mean, the *entire* village of Threadbare has been in such a tizzy over the poor girl's predicament."

Muncie wrote nothing on the chalkboard. "The Collectory already has this knowledge," he sighed.

"I'm just trying to set the stage for our friends here." Hugh winked at Zenith and Kreeble. "So, finally, bright and early this morning, Lorelei had her babies, but instead of the two predicted by the Threadbare midwife, there were three." He paused and leaned forward when he saw Muncie start to write.

Zenith leaned as well and saw the raven transcribe, "Lorelei Montgomery, wife of Yoseph, has born three children in the hamlet of Threadbare."

Hugh turned to Zenith. "And here's where it gets

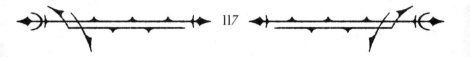

juicy. The first two are the spitting image of their father, large horns and all, but the third baby is born a ghost. And neither Yoseph nor Lorelei have any ghosts in their bloodline! So, of course, Yoseph has accused his wife of being untrue, and all eyes have turned toward the village smithy, who is half-ghost on his mother's side. But there are at least five other likely suspects—"

"Nonsense!" croaked Muncie, as he dropped the chalk onto the desk. "A *ghost* baby, Hugh? I ask you for knowledge, and all you give me is superstitious drivel!"

"These are the Details that the Seeker has found," replied Hugh, adopting his brother's formal tone.

"And where did you find them? In the Rolling Thunder Tavern? Did your lowlife pals give you these 'Details'? Did you even go see Lorelei for yourself? Or did you rely on 'eyewitness accounts' as you like to do?"

"Of course I saw her." Hugh averted his eyes and fiddled with his scarf. "I definitely saw the three babies. Although the ghost one didn't photograph that well."

"So, you saw a blurry photograph while you were

carousing." Muncie erased the word *three* from the chalkboard with the tip of his wing. "And one of your fellow ne'er-do-wells convinced you that some smudge was a ghost." He picked up the sparkly chalk and used it to write the word *two* in the erased space. Then he added the text, "Both babies are alive and healthy, and everyone's happy." The new words glowed bright white. Then the glow faded, and the new words became the same lime green color as the rest.

Hugh got very upset. "You can't just make a Revision and Addition like that!" But Muncie ignored him, grabbed the chalkboard in his beak, and hopped over to the Collectory. "That's not what happened!"

"It is now," replied Muncie. He opened his mouth to release the chalkboard, but instead of dropping to the ground, it remained suspended in the air. After hovering like that for a moment, it flew back to the Collectory, as if pulled by some invisible magnetic force. An empty branchlet caught the chalkboard and wrapped it in its threads. The chalkboard glowed white again briefly. Then it faded back to green, the same as all the rest.

"Did you see what he just did?" Hugh swung around to face Zenith and Kreeble. "He just wrote that poor ghost baby out of existence!"

"It didn't really exist, Hugh." Muncie hopped back over to his desk. "How can someone be born as a ghost? It's my sacred duty as Scribe to make sense of things when you return spouting this ridiculous garbage!"

Hugh turned back toward his brother. "So, ghosts are 'garbage,' are they? Well! I never knew my own brother was prejudiced against the noncorporeal!"

As the two ravens argued about what just happened, Zenith pulled Kreeble aside. "What just happened?"

Kreeble shrugged. "I suppose that the ghost baby is no longer around to cause trouble between Lorelei and Yoseph."

"No, okay, scratch that." Zenith shook his head.

Kreeble lifted a finger helpfully. "Scratch what, exactly?"

Zenith batted it away. "What has been happening *since we arrived*? Who exactly are these two?"

"They are the Scribe and Seeker of GrahBhag. They hold the History and the—"

"No, no, no. Stop. Drop all the titles and speak in plain Anglish. English! Speak in plain English. Ugh!" Zenith gripped his forehead and closed his eyes tight. Then, relaxing slightly but keeping his eyes closed, he began again. "The clumsy flying bird. Hugh. He goes around and finds out about things that are happening in GrahBhag, right?"

"That is correct."

"And then he flies back here and tells his brother, Muncie, who writes the news on little chalkboards and keeps them in this tree-type thing."

"The Collectory is more than a—"

"No. Stop. Please let me finish. So, Muncie writes it all down, but sometimes he doesn't believe Hugh. So, he'll alter the story and—"

"No." It was Kreeble's turn to interrupt. "These are not just stories. The Collectory holds the Truth of GrahBhag. There are the Details about its inhabitants, yes. But also the rules of the world itself. The sun sits in the sky because the Collectory says it is so. Up is up and down is down because the Collectory says it is so. If it is written in the Collectory, then it is true." She glanced over at the ravens. "And I suppose that if it is unwritten by the Scribe, then it becomes untrue."

"You're saying that whatever the Scribe writes on these chalkboards alters the reality of this entire world?"

"Yes," replied Kreeble. "Why do you find it necessary for me to confirm things right after I have told them to you?"

"I just find it hard to believe that reality itself can be changed with the stroke of a pen."

"The Scribe uses chalk, not a pen. And he is not the only one who edits the facts to his liking. We all shape our own reality by what we choose to remember or to forget. What is memory, other than a tale we tell ourselves about ourselves? A tale we amend, revise, and rewrite as the days and years roll by."

"Kreeble! I had no idea you were a philosopher," replied Zenith in a gently mocking tone.

"I am not. I am what your people call a gargoyle. I am honestly perplexed at how dull-witted you can be sometimes."

Zenith decided to end the conversation right there. He took a few steps toward the two bickering birds and cleared his throat loudly. "Excuse me, Scribe? Seeker?" When that didn't work, he yelled, "Muncie! Hugh!"

The ravens stopped quarreling and turned toward him. "Pardon my rude interruption," he continued. "But I was hoping you could share whatever Details you have about my sister, Apogee. I need to find her as soon as possible."

"Well?" challenged Muncie as he turned to face his brother. "Have you heard anything about this Firman's sister? Or were you too busy soaking up spirits and blathering on about ghost babies?"

"I was doing my job!" retorted Hugh. "I have to fly over the whole of GrahBhag looking for new Details. I'm only one bird. I can't be everywhere at once. Maybe if I had some help from you. Oh, but you can't fly, can you? You're stuck here on the ground with your useless wings and your pretty little chalk, writing down the Details that I bring you. So envious that I get to fly everywhere and see everything while you can't!"

Muncie hopped aggressively toward Hugh and squawked, "Get out!"

Hugh took flight and hovered above his brother as Muncie jumped up and tried to peck him.

"Get out of here! You lazy, brain-dead fool! Flight is wasted on you."

Hugh snickered and squawked as he gained altitude and flew away.

"*You're* the useless one!" continued Muncie. "Go back to the Rolling Thunder! Carousing is all you're good for!!"

The raven glared at the diminishing shape of his brother for a minute without speaking, then turned suddenly toward Zenith and Kreeble as if he'd forgotten they were there. The Scribe pushed the oversize spectacles up his beak with his wingtip. "Ah yes. The Firman. I must get your Details." He hopped over toward the desk, and Zenith followed closely behind him.

"You said you knew about my sister."

"And I would have if the Seeker had done his job." The bird patted Zenith on the shoulder. "Don't worry. Hugh will come crawling back in a day or two. I'm sure he'll have Details about her by then."

"A day or two?!"

"No reason to fret. It will take at least that long for you to read your book of science aloud while I transcribe every glorious word." The thought of it snapped the raven out of his foul mood. He looked down at the two small chalkboards lying on the desk.

"I'm going to need more slates." As he hopped over to the Collectory, he called back, "Make yourself comfortable, Firman. We're going to be here for a very long time."

Dumbstruck with frustration, Zenith stared blankly at Muncie as he retrieved more blank chalkboards with his beak. Kreeble climbed up the side of the desk, walked across the surface, and found a large pincushion. She removed the pins and sat down on it. "What are you doing?" asked Zenith.

"Making myself comfortable as the Scribe instructed."

"Do you really think I'm going to stay here and give that weird bird an endless physics lesson? When he can't tell me squat about Apogee?"

Kreeble shrugged. "What else is there to do? The Scribe and the Seeker are the only ones in all of GrahBhag who might be able to help you. How else can you possibly find your sister?"

Zenith had no answer. He had no idea what to do. But he knew he was not going to just sit there reading Apogee's textbook while Muncie took interminable notes on his magical chalkboards.

An idea popped into Zenith's head. He looked up

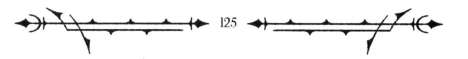

and saw Muncie hopping back toward them with a dozen slates crammed in his beak. Zenith leaned forward and called out to him. "You know, you might want to go get some more chalkboards. It's a pretty long book." Zenith tried to keep his upper arms still as his hands inched across the surface of the desk. He hoped that the desk's high backside would mask what he was doing.

It didn't. Muncie dropped the chalkboards from his beak. "What are you doing with that slate? What are you doing with my chalk? None but the Scribe may wield the enchanted chalk!"

"Well, I . . . ," Zenith stammered, then broke into a run. He was never any good at covering when he was caught.

The raven let out a cry of alarm and hopped after him. Zenith lost speed as he ran up the slope of the shallow valley toward the rock-lined rim. The enormous bird gained on him.

By the time he reached the rocks, the Scribe had halved the distance between them.

Zenith looked down at the sparkly chalk he'd swiped and snapped it in two. He raised the larger half over his head like he was playing fetch with a

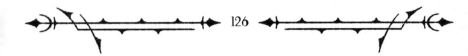

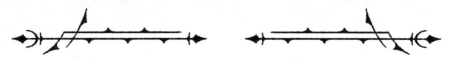

dog, and tossed it back into the valley past the approaching bird. Zenith didn't wait to see if his ploy worked. He ran as fast as he could away from the Collectory, slate and stub of chalk in hand.

18

Stolen Goods

ZENITH RAN TILL a little voice told him to stop. It wasn't the little voice inside his head. It was a little voice on his back. Kreeble had grabbed on to the backpack and was now dangling from the bottom of one of the straps. Zenith ducked into a copse of gnarled trees, and the gargoyle dropped the short distance to the ground.

"You are a most extraordinary creature," Kreeble said, trying to catch her breath. "One moment you have told the Scribe you will cooperate, and the next moment you have stolen his sacred tools and are running away."

Zenith peered between branches toward the Collectory, but the raven was no longer chasing them. He looked down at the gargoyle. "Why're you breathing so heavily when I was the one running?"

"Had to run to catch up with you before I could

jump onto your knapsack." Kreeble inhaled deeply. "You have very long legs." The gargoyle's breath slowed to normal after another moment. "Why did you defile the Collectory with your thievery? It is forbidden for anyone but the Scribe to wield the chalk and slates. How does committing this offense help us find your sister?"

"I'm not sure it will. But it's worth a shot." Zenith looked down at the stolen chalkboard and the nub of the enchanted chalk. There wasn't much room to write or much chalk to write with. He read "Zenith Maelstrom has a fourteen-year-old sister named Apogee," and used the chalk to add "and both of them are safe at home."

Zenith closed his eyes tight and braced himself for magical transport. None occurred. After a long moment he opened one eye and peered at the chalkboard. Then he scowled at it. And finally, he thrust it toward Kreeble. "Why didn't it send us back home?"

Kreeble read what he'd written. "I do not know." She pushed the chalkboard away gently. "It is not my place to know. As I said, the Scribe wields the chalk and slates. Perhaps the chalkboard's powers do not include passage between worlds."

Zenith let out a deep sigh of frustration and took another look at the chalkboard. He reluctantly wiped his failed Addition away with the hem of his shirt but left the Scribe's original message untouched. He studied the short text for a long time. He'd used up a good portion of the limited chalk on his first attempt and was unsure how many more chances he had before it crumbled away to nothing.

Finally, with some trepidation, he moved the stub to the end of the words "Zenith Maelstrom has a fourteen-year-old sister named Apogee" and added "and he knows exactly where she is right now."

The new words glowed bright white. Then the glow faded, and the Addition was the same aqua blue color as the rest of the message. Zenith turned toward Kreeble with a wild look in his eyes. "I need to get to a place called Stoating."

Celebration

"**THIS IS A** grave mistake. Stoating is a bad place. A dark place. A place of the Great and Holey Wurm! It is not a place to tread uninvited." Kreeble uttered these warnings into Zenith's ear as she dined on his earwax once again.

"You have a large appetite for someone who's so scared," Zenith remarked.

"I eat when I am nervous." Kreeble continued chewing in sulky silence.

Zenith followed the irregular, rust-colored stitches that Kreeble reluctantly told him led to Stoating. They'd backtracked toward the Collectory to pick up the trail, but hadn't been discovered by the Scribe. Zenith hated to admit it, but the gargoyle's doomsaying had spooked him at first. However, after what must've been at least two hours of uneventful travel up a gentle slope, he was less

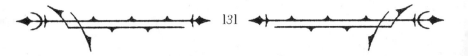

worried. The trip to Stoating had been remarkably easy so far.

The friendly terrain ended abruptly at the edge of a deep sandstone chasm. Here the haphazard trail of stitches grew rapidly in thickness before splitting into four strands and emerging from the gray rock to form the supports and frame of a fifty-foot rope bridge spanning the canyon.

This bridge looked nothing like the stereotypical rope bridges Zenith had seen in movies. The braided handrails and corresponding cords on the outer edges of the walkway were the only orderly parts of an otherwise anarchic jumble of ropes and cables that tied the frame together and formed the deck. It reminded Zenith of the chaotic web of a black widow spider. Was it designed to let travelers cross or to ensnare them?

He took a tentative step toward the bridge, cleared his throat, and then strode forward more forcefully. Upon reaching the edge of the cliffside, he paused. His stomach lurched at the sight of the jagged rocks on the canyon floor far below. There were large gaps in the webbing of the bridge's walkway, and Zenith pictured his foot slipping into one of them as he lost

his grip on the braided handrails and fell into the abyss.

"I do not like the look of this," said Kreeble, and gulped loudly in his ear.

"Bridges are built to be crossed," Zenith answered, sounding much more confident than he felt. Kreeble stopped eating and wrapped both her arms around his neck. After one last, long moment of hesitation, Zenith grabbed both handrails, reached over the first gap with his foot, and stepped onto the bridge.

The gargoyle gasped in surprise as the bridge dropped and swayed, its weave stretching under the weight of Zenith's body. Zenith tightened his grip on the handrails, expecting his feet to slip through the walkway's webbing and leave him dangling by his arms.

But the bridge held and settled. Zenith took another step forward, and it dipped and swayed, but not as dramatically as before. He made his way across the crevasse, step by fear-inducing step.

Wind rustled his hair and the tassels of his hoodie. As he approached the dead center of the bridge, a stronger gust threw him off-balance, his foot slipping

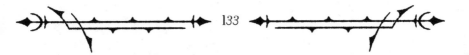

toward one of the gaps just as he'd imagined. Kreeble's arms tightened around his neck, almost choking him. He clutched the handrails, waiting for the wind to die down and the bridge to stop swaying. Then he continued across even more slowly than before.

Zenith finally made it to the other side. He stepped off the bridge and onto the opposite cliff, fatigued arms shaking from the exertion. He bent and rested his hands on his knees, taking a long, relieved breath. Kreeble gave him a reassuring pat on the shoulder, which he ignored, and after a moment more, he straightened up and strode away from the bridge without looking back.

Zenith quickened his pace. The trail on this side of the chasm moved downhill, but more importantly, he sensed that they were getting close to Apogee. Unfortunately, the nature of the terrain soon forced them to slow down again. The stitches led into a narrow ravine between two steep, sheer rock walls. The passage soon became so tight that Zenith wasn't sure he could squeeze through.

"I will repeat myself," said Kreeble. "I do not like the look of this."

"This time I have to agree with you." Zenith

kicked the gravel in frustration. "But I *know* Apogee is through here!"

A distant scream echoed through the narrow opening before them. "Is that your sister?" asked Kreeble.

"I don't know, but I'm going to find out."

He took off the backpack, turned sideways, and shuffled forward. His belly and back scraped the rock walls. Kreeble perched on top of his head and peered forward. They must've looked ridiculous, but Zenith's sense of humor was dampened by the shrieking from up ahead. There were now three distinct voices. If one of them was his sister, she was not suffering alone.

The passageway reached its narrowest point. Zenith paused, and Kreeble hopped off his head. The little gargoyle had no trouble traversing the narrow space on her own. Looking back at him, she waved her hand. "Come on. It widens up ahead." She accelerated and disappeared around a bend. Zenith inched forward very slowly. He was certain he was going to get stuck. And then he *was* stuck. But after an initial moment of panic, he exhaled sharply, drew in his stomach, and wriggled through.

The gorge did widen slightly and ended just a few yards up ahead, where Kreeble stood waiting. Zenith opened his mouth to speak, but the gargoyle shushed him. She whispered, "This is Stoating," as she turned to peer around the rock face in front of her. Zenith joined her.

The stitches that had led them there ran downhill as the landscape opened up below into a flat plateau. The thread's color brightened from dull rust to blazing orange before the stitches and the gray sandstone terrain were both engulfed by a hardened layer of black volcanic rock. This place seemed an unlikely site for volcanic eruptions, but the faint smell of sulfur permeated the air, and there was ample geologic evidence of a tumultuous past. Eight pillars of the coarse black rock rose up in a circular configuration around the outer edges of the encrusted ground, as if a synchronized eruption of lava had instantly cooled and hardened. At the top of the circle, there was a ninth formation unlike the others. The vibrant orange stitches reappeared at the base of this column and wound their way up around its exterior before the entire pillar terminated in a diagonal slice that left the outcropping half as high as the other eight.

The orange stitches emerged from the center of the rock, forming three cryptic symbols on the otherwise glossy obsidian surface of the pillar's diagonally exposed interior. Zenith recognized these symbols; they had been branded into the face of the old woman who warned him not to oppose the Wurm.

Zenith shook his head to clear it and looked at the ninth pillar again. There was a slightly elevated area in front of it that was reminiscent of an altar. This was a place for gatherings. For rituals.

This was no great insight, since there was an extravagant celebration going on at that very moment. A dozen tables draped in tattered animal pelts had been set up on the volcanic rock within the ring of the nine pillars. Several formally dressed creatures sat at each. Creatures with too many limbs and too many eyes. Some of them furry, some fleshy, some covered in scales. The things that came the closest to human form were the members of a musical quartet performing in the center of the party. The musicians' tuxedoed bodies were humanoid, but the similarity ended at their shoulders. For above their neatly pressed bow ties emerged the heads of rats, with gleaming, unblinking black eyes and protruding

yellow incisors. The drummer kept the rhythm on a booming kettledrum, while the other three used their ragged claws to poke and pluck at captive bobcats, creating mournful music out of the cats' howls. These were the sounds that Zenith had heard as he made his way through the narrow canyon.

Zenith turned away from the sadistic quartet, but was confronted with acts of cruelty wherever he looked. Many of the "dishes" being served still wriggled pitifully on the diners' plates. One lavishly dressed guest's fur coat wouldn't stop chittering, no matter how many times the wearer wrung its scrawny neck. Two other partygoers toasted each other, then tossed their effervescent beverages onto a third. Judging by that guest's screams, the fizzing liquid wasn't champagne.

It was too much to take in all at once, and Zenith wanted nothing more than to look away. But one thing kept his eyes riveted on the celebration—one creature in a cage.

Apogee.

Rescue

RELIEF WASHED OVER Zenith at the sight
of his sister. From a distance, she appeared to
be okay. It was quite a distance, however. True
relief would only come after he'd seen Apogee up
close, freed her, and taken her away from this grue-
some place.

Zenith bent as low as he possibly could and crept
quickly downhill toward the nearest of the volcanic
pillars. He plastered his back up against its outer side,
the column of rock being just wide enough to hide
him, and waited for a sign that he'd been spotted. But
the noise of the party went on uninterrupted. The
only sound of alarm came from the frightened gargoyle crouched at his feet.

"What are we doing?" whispered Kreeble.

"We're rescuing my sister," Zenith whispered
back. "You know, the human girl in the cage, who

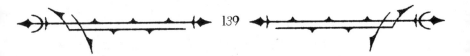

looks like me? Did you think I was going to just sit here and watch her be tortured or eaten by these monsters?"

"Why do you think that your kind is so appetizing? I, for one, would never—"

"Can we discuss this later? Like, *after* I've saved Apogee and we're out of this nightmare?"

Without waiting for an answer, Zenith darted from behind the pillar and ran to the next one. Kreeble followed as quickly as her little legs would carry her. After a shorter pause, Zenith moved again, and the gargoyle did likewise. But in her haste to keep up, Kreeble tripped on the uneven terrain and fell to the ground with a loud "Oof!"

The sound attracted the attention of one of the waitstaff, who turned to see Kreeble lying on her side in plain sight. The gargoyle had transformed into stone, her legs bent and arms outstretched. Her mouth was frozen in a fearsome growl. It was as if she'd just toppled off her column in Whichway Woods.

The server strode over and looked down at Kreeble, its four hands on what must have been its hips. Zenith pressed his body into the pillar, willing the waiter to keep all three of its eyes on Kreeble.

With a weary sigh, the server picked the stone gargoyle up off the ground and placed her on an empty table nearby. It rotated Kreeble one way and then the other, then slid a vase of wilting flowers close beside her. Apparently satisfied with this centerpiece arrangement, the waiter resumed its duties.

As soon as the waiter had moved on, Kreeble came to life, her outermost layer of stone bursting into dust. She leapt off the table and scurried to join Zenith in his hiding place. He thought she looked rather smug for someone who'd almost gotten them caught, but he held his tongue.

Just as they'd snuck around the ring of beasts in Albert's cabin, they traveled in a counterclockwise direction around the perimeter of volcanic pillars without further incident and stopped behind the one closest to Apogee. She was attended by a creature with the body of a blobfish, the eyestalks of a slug, and the tentacles of an octopus, one of which gripped his struggling sister through the bars of her cage. Zenith's first impulse was to rush out and punch the thing in its eyestalk, but he paused long enough to see that the slugtopus wasn't hurting Apogee. It was dribbling ink from its slimy mouth onto one tentacle

and then using the ink to draw something on Apogee's face. In a moment it finished and, with a deep bow to Apogee, it oozed away backward for a few feet, then turned to go. Zenith watched it pass the next nearest column of rock, squelch its way up onto the altar, and stop before the ninth pillar. It began tracing one tentacle along the three orange symbols in ritualistic repetition.

Zenith leaned out from behind the stone and whispered, "Apogee," as loudly as he dared.

Apogee looked over her shoulder, and her eyes went wide. "Zenith!"

Zenith ducked out of sight at the sound of his own name. The slugtopus turned its eyestalks their way. It stared intently at Apogee, who in turn stared intently at her feet. After a seemingly endless moment, the slugtopus turned back to the pillar and resumed its ritual. Zenith kept his head hidden but risked another whisper. "Are you okay? Are you hurt?"

"No. Just a little dirty. And inky," she whispered back.

Zenith chanced a glance from behind the pillar and saw what the slugtopus had drawn on her. She was covered from head to toe in more of those

cryptic symbols. The three on her forehead matched the three on the ninth pillar.

"What are you doing here?" she asked.

"A popular question." Zenith looked down to where Kreeble was hiding between his legs.

Apogee was incredulous. "Have you made a friend in here?"

"More like a business partner."

The gargoyle curtseyed quickly toward Apogee and tugged on Zenith's pant leg. "We need to leave," Kreeble whispered.

Zenith turned back to his sister. "We've got to find some way to bust open this cage. And do it quietly."

"Oh, you can try busting it loudly." The tip of her tongue protruded from between her lips as Apogee aimed her heel and gave the cage three loud kicks. Zenith ducked as the slugtopus turned its eyestalks again. It emitted a guttural hiss, but didn't leave its post. "I've been trying since they put me in here. It's unbreakable, and everyone knows it."

"Okay, okay," Zenith whispered sharply. "Don't be so loud! Let's try to keep everyone from finding out that your brother's crashed the party." They sat in silence for a few seconds. "I guess we'll have to

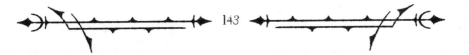

pick the lock. You used to be good at that back when you were fun. Or better yet, steal the key. Does that slugtopus have it?"

"You need tools to pick a lock. All we've got is chewing gum. And no, that whatever-you-called-it doesn't have the key. I haven't seen a key." Apogee let out a long sigh. "Why did you come after me?"

"What was I supposed to do? Abandon you here?"

Apogee gestured to the symbols on her body. "Obviously they have something big in store for me. When they open the cage, I'll make my escape."

"That's a crap plan, Apogee, and you know it. You're going to fight your way to freedom through this crowd of creeps? On your own? Why? Because you're too proud to let your little brother help?"

"Because I don't want to get my little brother killed," growled Apogee. "I'm your big sister, and *I* look after *you*. It doesn't work the other way around."

Zenith scowled and scratched the side of his head, but said nothing.

Apogee continued in a gentler voice. "Is that what this is all about? The pond? Just because I saved you then doesn't mean you need to save me now. I—"

"*Saved* me?" Zenith blurted out, his face red. He

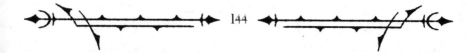

paused to gain control of his voice, but he did not gain control of his anger. "That's not how I remember it. I would've won if you'd kept quiet. But instead, my own sister rooted against me."

Apogee was taken aback. "What? Zenith, you're confused. I didn't—"

"Confused, huh? So, you didn't yell at me to stop me from winning?"

"No, I yelled, but it wasn't to—"

"I didn't need you butting in then, and I don't need you bossing me around now. This place is too dangerous for me? *You're* the one in the cage. *You're* the one who's about to be made into roast human. Or maybe they plan to eat you raw. Sushi style. While you're still alive so you'll be extra fresh."

"That is not the plan," said Kreeble very quietly. "I should have realized before. This place. The season. But it occurs to me only now."

"What are you talking about?" snapped Zenith. He didn't want the gargoyle interrupting when he'd finally gotten the chance to uncork all the anger he'd bottled up for so long.

"The Merging. This is a Merging ceremony. Your sister is to become one with the Holey Wurm."

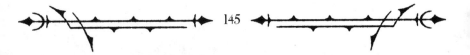

"Wait, what?" asked Apogee. "What the heck does that mean?"

"Are you talking about a wedding?" demanded an incredulous Zenith. "Are you telling me the Wurm rules this place, but it still can't get a date? It has to resort to kidnapping?"

Kreeble closed her eyes tightly. "You use so many words, but so few of them make sense to me. If you would only listen."

Zenith looked from the gargoyle to his sister and back again. "Merging, wedding, whatever you call it. Let's just get out of here before it begins."

Loud chanting interrupted their discussion. The three of them turned toward the sound, as did every other creature in attendance. The slugtopus stood before the ninth pillar, waving its tentacles slowly above its head. The intonations flowed from its ink-stained mouth.

"Too late," whispered Kreeble. "The Holey Wurm has arrived. The ceremony has begun."

The Great and Holey Wurm

THE SLUGTOPUS AT the altar stopped its incantation and bowed deeply till its head touched the ground. The guests and serving staff fell to their knees, if they had knees, and did the same. Even Kreeble put her head down. Only Zenith and Apogee were left standing.

A short, stout troll dressed in a white satin robe appeared from behind the ninth pillar and faced the prostrate crowd from the front of the altar. His skin was gray and heavily wrinkled. His white hair was long and framed the symbol burned into the skin on his high forehead. He held a thick leather-bound book in one long-fingered hand, while the other hand gently swung a small incense burner on a short chain. The smoke was dark, and the smell acrid. The troll's voice

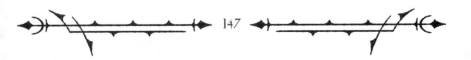

was low and booming. "Bow," he commanded unnecessarily. "Bow before That which is! That which is Everything and Nothing. Everyone and No One." He reached the stone altar and stopped. "Bow before Its Allfullness. Bow before Its Noneness. Bow before the Great and Holey Wurm!" The troll dropped to his knees next to the slugtopus and bowed until his head grazed the ground.

A cold gust of air stung Zenith's face. He lowered his head but didn't avert his eyes. A figure shrouded in a blood-red cloak embroidered with the same black symbols that adorned Apogee floated forward from somewhere unseen onto the altar. A contradictory mix of awe and revulsion overcame Zenith. Part of him wanted nothing more than to cower on the ground with the others, but curiosity and compulsion kept him from doing so.

From the front, the cloaked creature appeared to be about seven feet tall, and appeared to possess human proportions. However, a glance at its side revealed a bulky back end that trailed on for far too long. The shape of the Wurm reminded Zenith of a Centaur. But the comparison fell apart when, with a wipe of his watering eyes, he spotted the Wurm's

spindly, spidery legs scuttling under the bottom of the elongated cloak. They were the size and shape of Shlurp's nine legs, but this creature had nine times nine legs. Or maybe nine times ninety-nine. There were too many legs to count. A revolting number of legs.

The same spindly shapes played the part of the Wurm's fingers, a dozen or so poking out of each sleeve. Zenith half expected the same shapes to form the creature's face, but the hood of the cloak concealed its entire head. Zenith was grateful it did.

The Wurm came to a stop next to its two minions. Without ever raising its head, the slugtopus oozed away from its master, leaving a gelatinous residue behind. The troll rose to his feet, gripped the black velvet bookmark protruding from the middle of his book, and used it to open the tome to the desired passage. His eyes never left the page as he read out loud to the assembled guests, who kept their faces pressed to the ground.

"Hear me, unworthy. For the time of the Merging is nigh. Let the One of Age come forward. So that she might be consumed by Its Noneness. Become full in Its Allfullness. Let the One come forward so

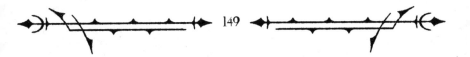

that the Great and Holey Wurm may merge with her and become the One True One." The troll kept his eyes averted, but gestured toward Apogee with an outstretched hand, and Zenith, peeking from behind the pillar, saw that he had a key dangling from a red ribbon tied around his thick wrist.

"There's the key we've been looking for," whispered Zenith.

Apogee looked at him with worry. "You don't know that. That key could be for anything."

Zenith kept his gaze on the troll and rubbed his scar.

"Zenith. I don't want you doing anything rash."

"And I don't want to be brother-in-law to the Wurm thing in the red cloak." He bent his legs like a runner before a race and wiped the nervous sweat from his brow.

"Zenith, stop. We'll come up with something else. Whatever it is you think you need to prove, fighting that troll isn't the way to do it. Please! You're too smart to be so stupid."

Any doubt Zenith felt was swept away by a fresh wave of anger. Apogee's favorite insult always gnawed at him. He glared at his sister. "Be ready to run."

Zenith leapt from behind the pillar, and sprinted toward the altar. The cleric was immersed in his booming oration. He neither saw nor heard Zenith coming till the boy was almost upon him. With a short, surprised cry, the creature swung the thick book up to block his attacker. Zenith caught it on the chin and floundered forward into the troll. Both of them tumbled to the ground, but Zenith ended up on top. He straddled the troll's belly and reached for the hand with the key, but the cleric wrapped both his arms tightly around his sacred book. The troll writhed back and forth while Zenith desperately tried to pry his arms apart and grab the key.

A low murmur rippled through the crowd as a few of the supplicants raised their heads slightly to see what was going on. Many more of them kept their faces planted firmly against the ground, however. And none of them made any move to intervene.

"Zenith! Zenith! ZENITH!" He could hear the rising panic in his sister's voice. Zenith dug his fingernails into the troll's arms, hoping that the pain would make the creature shift his wrists and give him a chance to grab the key.

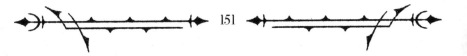

The thick-skinned troll just snarled and tightened his grip on the book.

The brute was stronger and tougher than Zenith. How was he supposed to beat him? Tickle him to death?

"Zenith Maelstrom. Get over here. *Now*." The change in tone made Zenith pause. His sister's voice was calm, firm, and (somehow) physically closer. He stopped struggling with the cleric and looked over his shoulder. Apogee stood halfway between him and the open door of her cage. She raised her hand toward him. "C'mon, Nit. We got to go."

Zenith stood up. The troll growled and scuttled away. Zenith took a step toward his sister. "How did you . . ." Apogee came toward him, then stopped abruptly. Her gaze left his face and settled on something behind him. Her eyes grew wide and vacant.

A chill ran through Zenith's body as he turned to face the Wurm. All he could hear was the sound of its countless legs skittering across the rocky ground as it approached. All he could see was the blood-red cloak as its massive body halted within inches of his own. All he could feel were its spidery fingers as it seized his shoulders.

The Wurm lifted Zenith off the ground until they were face-to-face. Except the Wurm had no face. Zenith was looking into the hood of the cloaked creature, but he saw nothing. The blackness was deep and wide and empty, and yet it was rushing toward him, or he was falling toward it, or neither of those things were true.

The warmth. The warmth was true. The air around the Wurm was so cold, but the air from inside its deep, dark hood was wonderfully warm. Zenith felt the warmth on his face. He felt the warmth in his mind. The warmth promised comfort. Safety. Nothingness. All he wanted was to be a part of the warmth. To be one with the warmth. To be melted. To be burned away. Any thought of his sister or of escape vanished.

And then thought itself was gone.

The Pond

ENDLESS, THOUGHTLESS WARMTH embraced him and then withdrew, abandoning him to a cold, indifferent darkness. Tendrils of tangled thought began to bathe his blank mind. Zenith recognized this darkness, knew this fog of thoughts. He wished it were all just a figment of his imagination. But these images were true. And they were painful.

Zenith was playing hockey with Apogee and a group of their friends on the frozen pond in Kalikov Park. The score was tied, but no one really cared who won. They were all having a good time, goofing around and laughing. Zenith liked this part of the day. This was before things went wrong. He'd chosen to forget exactly how things went wrong. But now he was remembering.

He remembered how he spotted the small crack

in the ice before anyone else, but chose to ignore it. How he stayed behind when the others saw the crack for themselves and retreated from the ice. How he razzed them for playing it safe.

Zenith remembered how, just when he was about to pack it in himself, Kevin Churl appeared, challenged him to a game of one-on-one, and called him Nit. Zenith tolerated his sister's use of that nickname, but he wasn't going to let Churl get away with using it. Zenith swore he'd wipe the floor (or ice) with him. Apogee pleaded with both of them to stop. She told Zenith he was "too smart to be so stupid." But he was too stubborn and prideful to be swayed.

Kevin played rough, and Zenith responded in kind. The fateful moment came. The game was tied, and time was almost up. Zenith had gotten the puck and was heading toward Kevin's goal when Churl tripped him with his stick. Zenith slid on his stomach across the ice but got back up quickly and chased after Kevin as he skated toward Zenith's net. *This* was when Apogee screamed, not before Kevin tripped him, but after. Not when he was about to win, but when he was about to put himself in danger. She cried, "Zenith! No!" Kevin turned at the sound

of Apogee's voice and raised his stick in self-defense. Zenith lunged at him and collided with the stick's blade, tearing open a deep gash in his own temple. A second later Zenith hit Kevin, knocking him down, smacking his own forehead on the ice, and sending them both sliding out to the center of the pond.

He blacked out for a second or two, and when he came back, Churl was on top of him, pinning Zenith's arms with his knees. But instead of triumph, he saw worry on Kevin's face. Zenith heard a loud crack, and they were both plunged into the freezing water as the ice broke around them.

The cold made Zenith gasp. He quickly closed his mouth, but the icy water had entered, and air had fled. He struggled to reach the surface, but the weight of his wet jacket dragged him down. The little bit of oxygen left in his lungs was about to run out. His vision blurred. He lost consciousness a second time.

Suddenly, there was a hand on his hood. Kevin pulled him to the surface. Zenith spat up water and gasped for breath. He took a swing at the boy before he realized that Kevin was trying to save him, not continue their fight. Churl helped him over to the

edge of the hole. They both tried to pull themselves out of the water. Neither of them could do it.

As both boys flailed, Apogee came crawling slowly into view. She was on her belly, sliding toward them across the perilous ice. Her feet were held by one of his friends, whose feet were held by another friend, whose feet were also held. His sister had led their friends to form a human chain to save him and Kevin.

Churl boosted him up as Apogee pulled on his arms, and then Zenith was out of the water. He crawled alongside the bodies of his friends toward the safety of the shore. Churl followed. Dry jackets were thrown over both of them, but they did nothing to stop Zenith's body from shivering. And the concern of his friends and sister did nothing to stop the shame and humiliation Zenith felt for how recklessly he'd behaved.

The Merging

SCREAMING. THE SOUND of screaming filled Zenith's head. For a moment he was grateful. The sound drowned out the painful sense of shame. But then the screaming became so loud that it itself became painful. He didn't want to think about the agony of the person producing such an ear-splitting noise.

"Apogee!" The thought was sharp, and it brought him wide awake. He sat up quickly, his eyes wide but unseeing. When they finally focused, Zenith didn't like what they saw.

He was locked inside his sister's cage, and she was free of it. But she wasn't free. The slugtopus had its tentacles wrapped around Apogee as she struggled in its grip. Beside them on the altar stood the troll, reading from his book. The screaming made it impossible for Zenith to hear what the repugnant creature was saying.

The sound was not coming from his sister, as he'd feared, but rather from a terrific wind that swirled around the circle of pillars and rushed into the Wurm's empty hood. The fiend stood on the altar with its arms upraised and its elongated backside spiraling out behind it. The size of its cowl gradually expanded as the wind grew stronger. The cleric turned the page of his book and gave the slugtopus a nod as he continued to read. The slugtopus started to uncoil its tentacles little by little, allowing the wind to slowly draw Apogee toward the gaping maw of the Wurm.

The dizzying blackness, the seductive warmth of the creature's empty gaze had engulfed him, burned him away to nothing. And yet the Wurm had only been toying with him, using its power to distract and disable him. Zenith was certain that its plan for Apogee was far more sinister. He doubted that Apogee would even exist once the Merging was complete, certainly not in any form that Zenith would recognize as his sister.

He grabbed the bars of the cage and shook and strained with all his might. He searched the bottom of the cage, desperate for anything that might help

him escape. What he found was Kreeble, pulling on his pant leg. When she saw she had his attention, the gargoyle scrambled up his body to her usual spot on his shoulder. Zenith was outraged.

"LET ME GUESS!" he shouted so that he could be heard over the tremendous wind. "YOU EAT WHEN YOU'RE NERVOUS!" He grabbed the gargoyle and tried to pluck her off, but she held firmly to his shirt collar.

"I want to talk, not eat!" She spoke directly into his ear, and Zenith could hear her quite well despite the wind. "I can get you out of here!"

Zenith let go of her. "HOW?"

"Your sister figured out how. Watch." Kreeble scrambled down his body and squeezed through the bars of the cage. The little gargoyle stuck one clawed finger into the lock and, with only a few moments of fiddling, had the cage door open. As Zenith stepped out of the cage, she scrambled back up onto his shoulder.

"SO, WHEN WE WERE TALKING ABOUT PICKING THE LOCK, YOU DIDN'T THINK TO DO THAT THEN?"

"What do you mean? There were not multiple

locks from which to pick. The lock and cage were already selected for your sister."

Zenith opened his mouth and then shut it. There was no time to explain their latest misunderstanding. "WE NEED TO GRAB APOGEE AND GET OUT OF HERE! DO YOU THINK THOSE HANDY CLAWS OF YOURS ARE SHARP ENOUGH TO SLICE THROUGH THAT THING'S TENTACLES?"

"They are sharp enough, yes. But how would that help your sister? That would only quicken the Merging."

Zenith looked at his sister. Her eyes were closed, and her face turned away from the Wurm. She resisted with all her might, leaning back and digging her heels into the ground, but her efforts were for naught. The slowly loosening grip of the tentacles Zenith had foolishly suggested slicing was actually the only thing stopping his sister from being immediately swept into the cloaked vortex that was the Wurm.

The ritual must've demanded a slower pace. The slugtopus closely attended the troll, who continued reading from his book. Time was short, regardless. His sister had already been pulled more than halfway

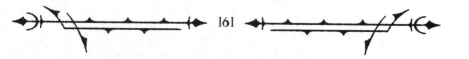

toward the Wurm. He thought about just running over there, grabbing Apogee, and yanking her out of the slugtopus's clutches. But then wouldn't they *both* be sucked into the whirlwind inside the red cloak?

No. *They* wouldn't.

Apogee was being drawn to the Wurm, her hair and clothes whipping around like she was in a hurricane, but its minions remained still and unaffected. Zenith looked down at his own clothes and saw that it was the same for him. The wind sounded incredibly powerful as it whipped past his ears, but it had no pull on him.

"WHY IS THE WIND ONLY AFFECTING APOGEE?"

"It is your sister's time to become one with the Wurm. It is no one else's time. Only the One of Age is drawn to the Merging."

If that was true, then Zenith supposed he could run right up to the Wurm without getting pulled inside. He could grab the gargoyle around the ankles and wield her sharp claws like a multibladed knife. But what would they be slicing at? The Wurm was mostly not there. Zenith could stab at its hands or feet; they at least appeared to be solid. But how many

of the hundreds of limbs would he need to hurt before the nothing inside the cloak took notice?

Apogee was only a few feet from the Wurm. Despite her efforts to look away, she must have glimpsed the void inside its head, because she now gazed into the expanding hood with wide, unseeing eyes. Her arms and legs were limp. Her resistance appeared to be at an end. The only thing holding her back was the slugtopus's tentacles. Zenith supposed it would release his sister when the ceremony concluded. And unfortunately, the troll had just turned to the final page of his book.

Zenith's overwhelming sense of shame came flooding back again. He'd behaved so badly that day on the pond that he couldn't face it. He'd turned away from the truth, revised, rewritten, and reordered events. Told a tale about himself that was more to his liking. Turned Apogee into a villain alongside Kevin Churl, when he should've thanked them both for saving him. Ever since, Apogee had made it her job to protect Zenith from his own reckless instincts. In return, he'd become bitter and resentful. And now he'd gotten her dragged into this treacherous world and screwed up their attempts to escape.

Zenith could see no way out. He could see no way to fight this baffling monstrosity and win. He could see no way to save his sister. She was "the One of Age," whatever that meant. She was the one Shlurp had chosen. And now the Great and Holey Wurm was going to swallow her whole.

This torrent of thoughts stopped, and Zenith's mind became calm and still for one long moment. He grabbed the backpack, thrust his hand into the large open pocket, and pulled out the chalkboard.

The troll finished reading and closed his book with a theatrical flourish. He bowed his head deeply, and the slugtopus followed suit as it unfurled the last bit of its tentacles from around Apogee's waist. The screaming wind grew louder.

Zenith read what was written on the chalkboard once more. "Zenith Maelstrom has a fourteen-year-old sister named Apogee, and he knows exactly where she is right now." How could he add to or alter what was written in a way that would save Apogee? He had a small amount of space, a small amount of chalk, and a small amount of time.

"Small . . . ," Zenith uttered. That was it! Zenith frantically grabbed his shirt hem and used it as a

makeshift eraser on the board, then cursed at himself as he wiped away more than he'd intended.

Apogee's hair and clothes continued to flutter furiously as the wind raged around her, but her limp body floated slowly toward the hooded vortex that was now as wide as she was tall. Was Apogee still resisting after all, or was the Wurm simply taking time to savor the moment? The rays of the late afternoon sun hit the ninth pillar, and the embedded symbols began to glow. The symbols on Apogee's forehead and the Wurm's cloak did the same.

Zenith opened the backpack's smaller pocket to grab the enchanted chalk, but he couldn't find it. He found the ballpoint pen. He found the pen again and again, but he couldn't find the chalk.

The glowing symbols on the rock and Apogee and the Wurm grew brighter and began to flash sporadically as his sister drifted closer to the vortex.

The wind grew even louder. Zenith cringed as he continued to search. He was about to upend the backpack and dump out all its contents when he remembered there was a third pocket on the backpack's side. He unzipped it and found the chalk.

The wind got louder. The bright light brighter.

Even with his face inches from its surface, Zenith could barely see the chalkboard. He lifted the small stub of iridescent chalk and rewrote the first part of the word he'd erased. He lowered the chalk and squinted at the board. Did the letters glow white like they were supposed to?

The whole world glowed white. The ungodly wind became a scream of agony.

Apogee's body warped and stretched and melted into the Holey Wurm.

Zenith cried out, unheard in the unearthly torrent of sound.

An instant later, the white light was gone.

The wind was gone.

Apogee was gone.

Birthday

SPOTS SWAM BEFORE Zenith's eyes. He bent his head and blinked rapidly. When his vision was clear, he looked down at the words on the chalkboard. They read "Zenith Maelstrom has a four-year-old sister named Apogee," and the word *four* was now the same aqua blue color as the surrounding words.

Zenith looked up to see the cloak of the Wurm twisting and convulsing like a bedsheet caught in a washing machine. The color of the material had darkened from bright red to mottled purple, as if it were bruised.

The troll and slugtopus raised their heads, and the rest of the assembled crowd soon followed. Their frightened faces and startled cries told Zenith that, whatever was happening to the Great and Holey Wurm, it was not a part of their ceremony.

With a piercing, multi-voiced screech, the Wurm stretched its hood up to twice its previous height, drawing the rest of its body up with it. Its fingers disappeared up its sleeves, and its multitude of legs thrashed wildly about before collapsing. A moment later the cloak crumpled, then billowed out, covering the legs like a shroud. But as it fell to the ground, Zenith watched in fascination as a bulge grew within the cloak, then pushed itself up toward the dark opening of the Wurm's hood.

The bulge emerged as the hood settled upon the ground. It rolled end over end past the troll and slug-topus and came to a rest with one final flop. It began to cry like a baby. Which only made sense, since it *was* a baby. Or rather, a young child.

The little girl reminded Zenith of a prized family photo that sat on their mantelpiece back home. The picture showed his sister with a party hat on her head and cake all over her face, tears streaming down her cheeks as she clutched her favorite blanket. Neither of their parents could recall what had upset her so, but they clearly remembered Apogee crying through most of that birthday party. She'd just turned four years old.

Exit

AFTER THE EXPULSION of Apogee, the color of the Wurm's cloak darkened further, from a bruised purple to a deep burgundy. Zenith had no idea whether this was a sign of recovery or further distress. Apparently, no one did. The slugtopus moaned and flailed its tentacles in despair, as the troll frantically thumbed through his book. The monstrous attendees gradually arose from their knees and inched toward their fallen master.

Young Apogee remained seated on her bottom, crying her eyes out. Zenith grabbed the backpack hastily and went over to her. "Be quiet, Apogee," he whispered. He gathered her now-oversize shirt up around her and hugged her to his chest. She was, once again, small for her age. Small for a four-year-old, but *really* small for a fourteen-year-old. Zenith paused at the thought. It was quite a bit easier to hold

her than it was to grasp the enormity of what he'd just done.

Apogee hit his cheek with her tiny fist. "Wha'd you do, 'Nit?"

"I was just asking myself the same thing."

"Change me back. Now!"

Zenith hugged his sister more tightly. "Shhh! I'll change you back when we're safe. Now keep it down, or you'll draw everyone's attention."

Ironically, it was her silence that drew everyone's attention. The moment Apogee stopped crying, the troll's face rose from his book and turned toward the two of them. He pointed with a trembling finger. "Heretics! Heretics! The Merging has been undone! They have defiled the Great and Holey Wurm and doomed us all!"

The mob of monsters scowled at Zenith and Apogee.

"The crowd's current emotion is rage!" shouted Kreeble. She was already back at the entrance to the ravine and was waving him on frantically. "Time to run!"

And Zenith did just that.

He could hear the hideous things growling

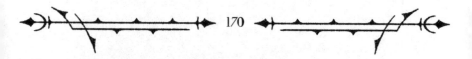

behind them, but he nonetheless concentrated on the uneven ground before him. One of them might catch Zenith and Apogee because it was simply too fast to outrun, but he didn't want to fail because he lost his footing. It was only after he'd cleared the volcanic rock and was back on the gray sandstone incline that he turned back.

The troll and the slugtopus had remained with the Wurm, but every other fiendish attendee was coming up fast behind them, teeth gnashing and claws reaching forward from the sleeves of well-pressed suits and silken blouses. Even the bobcats, whose screams had provided the party's music, had joined their rat oppressors in pursuit of Zenith and Apogee.

One impeccably dressed guest discarded its patent-leather loafers and began galloping on all fours. Or was it all fives? There was something odd about its gait, but its limbs were moving too quickly for Zenith to count or for the rest of the crowd to keep up. It broke away from the pack and gained on Zenith at a frightening pace.

Fright increased Zenith's own pace, and he sprinted the remaining distance to the ravine's narrow entrance. He frantically passed his sister through the

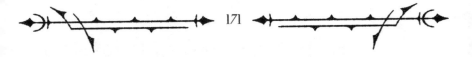

crevice to Kreeble, who couldn't handle the child's size or weight and promptly collapsed underneath Apogee. There was a loud roar close behind Zenith, and he whipped around to face his lead pursuer. The creature leapt at him, claws first. Zenith raised his backpack in front of his chest and blocked the fiend's attack. The force of the blow knocked Zenith off his feet and through the gap in the rock. He landed on his right shoulder and pulled his legs up to his chest just in time to avoid the second swipe from his foe.

Zenith scooted backward, away from the narrow fissure, as the growling ghoul stretched its arm forward, desperate to reach him. The rest of the horde soon joined, cramming the crevice with their menacing mugs, as claws and paws and tentacles struggled to grab hold of them.

But it was useless. Zenith, Kreeble, and Apogee could fit through the gorge's narrow passageway, but these larger creatures couldn't. They soon realized this themselves and backed away, snarling with frustration.

Zenith stood up and took a tentative step toward the crevice as his attackers continued their reluctant retreat. He looked beyond the crowd to where the troll

and slugtopus kept vigil by their incapacitated master. The color of the Wurm's cloak was unchanged, but now there was movement beneath it. The multitude of spindly legs had reappeared beneath the hem of the garment. Nine of those legs moved out from under the cloak completely, and even from a distance, Zenith recognized the loathsome thing. It was Shlurp.

Then nine more legs moved out to join Shlurp, and they were also Shlurp. Or rather, Shlurp's twin. Then a triplet joined them. And a quadruplet. And a quintuplet. Zenith could not think of the term for the sixth identical sibling. What he thought instead was *yuck* and *ugh* as Shlurps poured out from underneath the Wurm's robe. Zenith shuddered as he realized that the Wurm might be nothing more than a conglomeration of these odious creatures.

Then another thought occurred to him. *Those things will be able to fit through the narrow gorge very easily.* And as if they'd read his mind, the swarm of Shlurps stampeded toward them.

Tight Race

ENITH SIDESTEPPED QUICKLY through the narrow passage, paying no mind to the scrapes he earned for moving so fast. His only concern was for Apogee. He clutched his sister tightly against his chest, one hand on her head and one on her bottom. He'd covered her from head to toe with her oversize shirt for added protection. Apogee screamed and wriggled, and it was a challenge to keep her from banging her bundled head and the hand that held it against the rocks.

Finally, the trail widened. Zenith paused and looked back. He could hear the clamor of countless Shlurp legs skittering and scuttling along the rock wall behind them.

But Kreeble was the creature that he saw come running around the bend, carrying Apogee's backpack over her head. She tossed it to Zenith, waited

impatiently while he put it on, then clambered up his body and resumed her normal place on his shoulder.

"You were running, and now you have stopped," she said. "Time to start again."

He did as Kreeble suggested, running along the bottom of the widening canyon. Zenith focused on the path before him, but his ears were tuned to the sounds behind him. He was moving fast, but the terrible things were gaining ground.

Zenith made it to the other side of the gorge and ran up the hill to the rope bridge. He paused to catch his breath. Apogee was not nearly so light in his arms as when he'd first picked her up, and now he had the gargoyle and the backpack to carry as well. He looked down at the chasm and recalled how difficult it'd been to cross the bridge the first time, when he was less encumbered and much less exhausted.

Glancing back, he saw the swarm of Shlurps come pouring out of the distant ravine, blackening the rock face. Zenith fastened a knot at the bottom of his sister's shirt. He pulled the sleeves around his chest and cinched them behind his back, underneath the backpack. With Apogee pressed against his chest

in this makeshift knapsack, Zenith's hands were free. He grabbed the handrails and hurried across the bridge, avoiding the gaps and forcing himself to stop when the swaying became too violent.

Kreeble clutched his neck, whispering, "Careful, careful," repeatedly into his ear.

They were almost to the other side before Zenith said, "When we get across, I need you to use your claws to cut the supports of the bridge. Do you think you can do that?"

"I would rather use your long legs to carry me away as fast as you can."

"My legs are no match for those creatures' legs. They are going to catch us unless we stop them from following."

"Too late!" shrieked Kreeble.

Zenith looked back and saw a lone Shlurp scurrying across the bridge. The spider-like creature looked quite at home in the bridge's chaotic webbing, and the bridge barely swayed as the multilegged monstrosity scuttled toward them. With some difficulty, Zenith balanced on one leg and raised the other. When the thing came into range, he kicked it right in the center of its squishy body. The Shlurp sailed

over the side and down toward the rocks. The bridge swung violently from the force of his kick, but Zenith held on tight.

When the swinging stopped, Zenith hurried across the short section of the bridge that remained. He collapsed to his hands and knees, grateful for the solid ground. "Cut the ropes!"

Kreeble hopped off his arched back and ran to one of the four supports. Zenith had foolishly imagined the gargoyle slicing through each rope with one swipe of her sharp claws. Instead, Kreeble used them to saw back and forth against the thick braid. She made steady progress, but it was slow going. Meanwhile, more of the Shlurps arrived at the bridge and scurried across.

Zenith stood up and faced them. He took off the backpack and held it in his right hand, judging its weight. The thick physics book inside gave it some real heft. Apogee pushed herself away from his chest and looked up at her brother. "Put me down. Let me help," she demanded.

Zenith smiled at her. "It's okay, sis. If there's one thing I'm good at, it's hitting and kicking things."

He took Apogee's bundle and swung her around

so that she clung to his upper back, thereby shielding his sister from the approaching onslaught.

The Shlurps came across two, three, four at a time. Zenith swung his backpack at them like a wrecking ball. He punched them. Stomped them. Then kicked them. Whatever it took to stop them and send them sailing off the cliff.

Meanwhile, Kreeble finished cutting her way through the first two supports. One side of the bridge came away from the cliff and dropped, tilting to the left. Several Shlurps slid off the detached side and disappeared into the chasm. Apogee giggled with delight.

Kreeble scrambled over to the final two supports just as a fresh batch of Shlurps poured across the bridge. They rushed around the brave little gargoyle as she worked. "Ew, ew, ew," she protested as their multitudinous legs brushed against her.

Behind her, Zenith kept up his counterattack, swinging his backpack with a righteous fury. He glanced at Kreeble and was relieved to see her finish with the third support and start on the final rope securing the bridge in place. He could maintain this manic pace for a few more minutes at the most. Then

he would be spent, and they would be overtaken. He remembered how horrible it was to have one of these slimy creatures crawling over his body. What would it be like to be buried under a horde of them?

With a yelp of delight, Kreeble severed the final rope. The end of the bridge dropped and slammed against the cliff wall on the opposite side of the gulf with tremendous force, sending several Shlurps plunging into the abyss. Zenith let out a celebratory whoop as he sent the last Shlurp on his side flying through the air with one final, triumphant swing of the backpack.

The few creatures that had, improbably, remained clinging to the detached bridge climbed back up the far cliff's edge to rejoin the still sizable group congregated there. Zenith chuckled as he watched them crawling over one another with frustration.

But no, that was wrong. They *were* crawling over one another, but it was with a specific purpose in mind. After a moment, their intent became clear to him. The Shlurps were joining their sticky bodies together to form their own bridge across the crevasse.

The swarm's plan was clear to Kreeble as well. She pulled on Zenith's pant leg. "It is time to start

running yet again." She climbed up to his shoulder once more. "It is downhill from here. Perhaps you can move fast enough to outrun them."

Perhaps, thought Zenith. Perhaps the three of them could make it downhill. Perhaps they could even make it back to the Collectory. But could they really make it all the way back through Whichway Woods and up the other hill to escape GrahBhag before they were caught by these nasty, clever creatures? His instinct was to run, but he decided to use his brain instead of his feet.

"We must go," Kreeble implored. "Move as fast as possible!"

Zenith unzipped the backpack.

"What are you doing?"

Zenith brought out the chalkboard and the sparkly chalk. "Moving as fast as possible."

"That is the exact opposite of what you are doing!"

Zenith ignored Kreeble and stared at the chalkboard, thinking about how to write out the idea he had with as few words as possible to preserve space on the board as well as the stubby piece of enchanted chalk.

After "Zenith Maelstrom has a four-year-old sister named Apogee, and he knows exactly where she

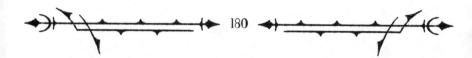

is right now," he added "Zenith commanded and rode upon the fastest creature in GrahBhag."

As the letters began to glow white, Zenith swung his sister's makeshift knapsack around and clutched her to his chest, half expecting to magically pop into a saddle upon some peculiar, equine creature. When that didn't happen, he looked at the chalkboard again. The new words had turned the proper color, but nothing had happened.

"Have you written your last words and wishes on that slate?" asked Kreeble. "Do you plan to end yourself?"

Zenith didn't have the heart to correct her. Besides, he wasn't so sure what she'd said was wrong. If they didn't get out of there, what he'd written *might* be his last words.

He glared at the half-completed bridge of Shlurps. Their black bodies were butted up against one another, their legs interlaced. Some of the creatures had crawled down the cliff's wall to form an arched support for the deck that a second group was quickly creating to span the chasm. A third group sat on the far cliffside, waiting not-so-patiently for their siblings to complete the bridge so they could rush across it.

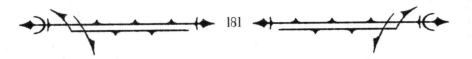

"Have you decided to let the children of the Wurm take you?" Kreeble's voice had grown more anxious. "Or perhaps you are thinking of jumping. If that is the case, please alert me beforehand, and I will climb off your shoulder."

Zenith was about to respond when a loud shriek split the air. The hairs on the back of his neck stood up. He knew that sound. It sounded like a bird of prey about to attack.

Flight

THERE WAS A second loud shriek, but this one was clearly a cry of laughter. The laugh ended with a loud shout of "There you are!" Zenith looked up to see Hugh, Seeker of GrahBhag, circling overhead. The raven dove sharply toward the cliff's edge. The force of his own landing seemed to surprise Hugh. He staggered past them and slammed into the hillside.

Hugh brushed the dirt off his body. "Sorry, Firman Zenith, but I had the most devilish time finding you. The hills around Stoating are a bit confusing to navigate."

"Why were you looking for us in the first place?" asked Zenith.

"A loyal servant can sense when his master needs him."

"Master?" Zenith looked down at the chalkboard

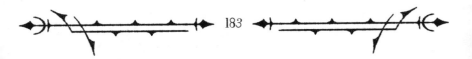

and read what he'd written. "So, *you're* 'the fastest creature in GrahBhag'?"

Hugh puffed out his feathered chest. "Well, I *have* won the Race of the Seven Stitches for three years running, so I think I can rightfully claim that title."

"And you're under my command?"

"Of course. I cannot think of why or how it is so, but I know it to be true."

"No reason to think too hard about it," said Kreeble as she looked back toward the bridge of Shlurps. "Just fly us out of here, Seeker." She crawled up one of Hugh's legs.

"Get off me, vermin!" Hugh shook his leg till she fell. "None but Master Zenith tells me what to do."

"Fly us out of here," said Zenith. "All of us. Even the vermin."

"As you command," Hugh said in a servile tone. The bird bowed his head low, and Zenith climbed onto his huge back. He slid the sparkly chalk into his front right jeans pocket, shoved the chalkboard into his hoodie's pouch, tightened Apogee's knapsack, and put the backpack on. Kreeble clambered up to her traditional place on his shoulder.

Zenith grabbed the two ends of Hugh's long

green scarf and held them like reins. He gave them a soft tug and yelled, "Giddyup!"

"What's that?" Hugh raised his head. Zenith nearly toppled off the bird, but his hold on the scarf saved him. While he struggled to right himself, the Shlurps completed their bridge. The waiting group of Shlurps started to scramble across it. "I'm sorry, Master, but I don't understand the Firman word you just used. Is that Anglish?"

"Just go! Go! Get us out of here!" screamed Zenith as the terrible things closed in on them.

"Fly! Fly! Fly!" chirped Apogee.

"Oh, of course," Hugh calmly replied. With a single flap of his enormous wings, they were up in the air.

Zenith wasn't prepared for the force of the take-off. His upper body slammed down into Hugh's neck, and his face was buried in feathers. They were the softest thing he'd hit his head on since arriving in GrahBhag. Zenith thought about keeping his face buried there and taking a little break. But his smothered sister was beating on his shoulders with her tiny fists. As he sat back up, she gasped and said, "Whad the heck, 'Nit!" She fixed him with a withering gaze.

Apogee might have lost most of her size and stature, but she'd kept the full strength of her scornful stares.

"Sorry, sis." Zenith grabbed the scarf a little tighter and leaned to the left to peer around Hugh's giant head. The bird was flying in circles above the hills of Stoating. "What're you doing?"

"A very good question," replied Hugh. "What *am* I doing, Master?"

Zenith let out an exasperated sigh. "Fly us to Whichway Woods, the quickest way you know how!"

"As you command." Hugh turned and plunged back toward the bridge of Shlurps.

"What're you doing now? Why are you diving?" screamed Zenith.

"There's a lovely little updraft in this gully. It will give us a delightful push to speed us on our way."

Sensing their approach, the bridge of beasts quickly reconfigured itself, and a thirty-foot-high tendril of Shlurps arose, reaching toward them as they descended. In a moment it would coil itself around the bird's body and pull them all down into the abyss.

Zenith groaned. "No, no, no, no."

The Shlurp at the top of the tendril spread its

nine legs wide and strained toward them as the bird dove directly toward it.

At the last moment, Hugh caught the updraft and soared skyward, swiping the top Shlurp as they rocketed past the nasty devils.

Zenith looked over his shoulder. The collision with Hugh had thrown the tendril's acrobatic act off-balance and destabilized the entire bridge. The horrid creatures broke apart and plummeted into the chasm. Zenith watched till the last one was lost in the shadows from the setting sun.

When he finally faced forward, a relieved Zenith could see the towering shape of the Collectory ahead and to the right. Farther off in the distance was a mass of green that must have been Whichway Woods. Their salvation was within sight.

Hugh suddenly stopped flapping, and they dropped fifty feet before he began again. The bird struggled to regain the lost altitude, but Hugh's flight was erratic. Something was wrong.

"What're you doing?" Zenith asked again, this time with concern rather than irritation.

"Apologies, Master, but I think we have an unwanted passenger."

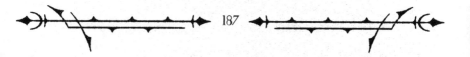

Zenith leaned and peered down the length of Hugh's massive frame. The Shlurp from the top of the tendril had managed to grab the bird after all. As Zenith watched, it climbed up the bird's belly and the underside of his neck, then tried to cover Hugh's eyes with its awful body. Hugh swung his head from side to side to keep the thing from blinding him. He ceased flapping so he could use his wings in a futile attempt to knock the creature off his head. Zenith's stomach lurched as they plunged toward the ground. He grabbed Apogee and Kreeble, wrapped his body around them, closed his eyes, and braced for impact.

Crash

THEY CAME DOWN in the valley of the Collectory. Hugh's immense body took the brunt of the crash, but the force was great enough to throw Zenith, Apogee, and Kreeble from the bird's back. Zenith felt the backpack and his sister's bundle fly away from his body. The moments after were a jumble. Bouncing and tumbling along the ground. The noise of Apogee crying. Or laughing. A green blur as something flew past his face. His own shoe? A white flash from the branches of the Collectory.

Zenith came to rest on his back with a few scrapes and bruises; his head was swimming, but nothing was broken as far as he could tell. He got up on his elbows and spotted Apogee sitting on her butt. Her oversize shirt was twisted and ripped. She looked bewildered, but appeared unharmed. Kreeble ran

around with the backpack, picking up the spilled contents. Hugh had a slight limp, but otherwise seemed physically intact. His emotional state was another matter.

"Where is it? Where is it?" His head swiveled as he hobbled about. "Where is it?"

The Shlurp was the only thing that appeared to be missing from the crash site, and Hugh was right to be worried. "Let's get back up in the air before we find out," Zenith said as he picked up his sister and ran back over to the panicking raven. Hugh kept looking about nervously.

"Thieves!" The scream made all of them flinch. Muncie came hopping toward them from across the valley.

Zenith hurriedly fastened his sister's torn shirt around his midsection as best he could. "Ignore your brother and get us back in the air. I command you."

The wild look in the bird's eyes diminished. "Yes, Master Zenith." He lowered his head.

"Criminals returned to the scene of their crime!" cried Muncie as he closed in. "Come to beg for mercy, eh? Too late! I've already written up a

scathing indictment and am about to send it off to the Inquisitor. However, if you return the chalkboard and the enchanted chalk, I *might* be persuaded to forgive your heinous misdeed."

"Sorry, Scribe," Zenith said as he climbed up onto Hugh's back. "But I still need them. There are some Additions and Revisions I've got to undo."

The sight of Zenith and the others astride his brother made Muncie stop short. "Hugh? What in the Name of the Wurm are you doing? You're not helping these outlaws, are you?"

"Sorry, Muncie," Hugh replied sheepishly. "No time to explain. Not sure I *could* explain. Forgive me." And with a mighty flap of his wings, they were up in the air once again.

"Traitor!" Muncie screeched from below as they flew away, his voice floating up to them even after he was out of sight. "I shall add your betrayal to the list of crimes for the High Court. Fly as far as you like! Hide in the dankest corner of the darkest tavern! Justice shall find y—*Squaaawk!*"

Hugh looked back at the pained sound from his brother. "What was that?"

"I don't know, but there's no time to find out,"

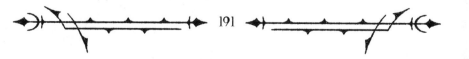

said Zenith. The sky was quickly turning the deep olive green of nightfall.

The forest came into view, and with it, Raggedy Albert's cabin. As they flew closer, the front door was thrown open and the giant rushed out onto the porch. With his button eyes turned skyward, Albert brandished an ax and yelled at them in his inscrutable language. Zenith didn't need Kreeble to translate. Albert's hostility was quite clear.

"That odd individual is trying to get our attention," said Hugh. "Is he a friend of yours?"

"Luckily, he's not," replied Zenith.

Hugh headed downward. "Shall I see what he wants?"

"No!" screamed Zenith and Kreeble. The bird regained the altitude he'd lost.

Zenith pointed past Albert and the forest. "Take us to the far side of Whichway Woods and land on that hillside."

"Hurry!" added Apogee.

"Well, yes. Of course, hurry," said Zenith.

"No." Kreeble placed her hands on his chin and swiveled his head around. "Really hurry."

Zenith saw what had so alarmed his sister and

the gargoyle. Muncie had made it up into the air and was gaining on them, flapping his hole-riddled wings madly to make them work.

Zenith tapped Hugh on his head. "I thought your brother couldn't fly."

"He can't," Hugh replied before looking back. "He can!" He let out one of his shrieking laughs and called out to Muncie as he approached. "Huzzah! Well done, brother! How in heaven's name did you manage to get up in the heavens?"

With a burst of manic flapping, Muncie closed the gap between them. Hugh whimpered at what he saw. The Shlurp had plastered its vile body on top of his brother's skull; its legs were wrapped tightly around the bird's spellbound eyes, under his chin, and were even inserted into the corners of his mouth. The invader opened Muncie's beak, and a foreign voice hissed, "All things are possible through the Wurm."

The Shlurp made Muncie flap his wings even harder. The raven rose up and then dove at them. Hugh dodged the attack, but Muncie's wing whacked Zenith. "C'mon, Hugh! You've got another race to win. Move!"

The two ravens traced an erratic path across the darkening sky over Whichway Woods. The Shlurp tried to knock Hugh out of the air, but the bird bobbed and weaved quite deftly.

Hugh's landing at the bottom of the hill was just as skillful, with none of his usual stumbling. Crises seemed to bring out the best in him. After briefly circling above them, the Shlurp used Muncie's body for one last lunge at them. Hugh shook his passengers from his back and then used *his* body to block the beast's attack. Zenith crouched protectively over Apogee and Kreeble as the two ravens rolled past them and came to a rest at the base of the hill.

The dark of encroaching night made the entangled birds into a confused mix of feathers, wings, beaks, and legs. For a moment all was still. Then there was a slight shaking of Hugh's head. But it wasn't Hugh. It was the Shlurp climbing out from beneath him. It staggered past the birds and wobbled toward them. Two of its legs seemed to be busted, but it had seven more, and it wasn't giving up.

With a weary grunt, Zenith hoisted his sister up over the shoulder that wasn't already occupied by Kreeble and ran uphill, following the stitches that'd

led him into this world and would hopefully show him the way out. He half expected the opening through which he entered GrahBhag to have vanished, but it and the other two openings were right where they should have been, a few feet in front of the steep cliff.

"If you are going to—" began Kreeble.

"Jump off the cliff, let you know ahead of time?" finished Zenith. "Nope. Not going over the cliff. Jumping in that hole."

Kreeble climbed down his body and peered into the hole at Zenith's feet. "A peculiar way to end things . . ."

"The only thing it'll end is our time in this horrible world of yours." Zenith tried to tie Apogee's bundle around his torso once again, but her torn shirt ripped some more, and he almost dropped her. He hugged her tightly and dropped the shirt instead.

"You are leaving? But what about our deal? I am guaranteed lifetime access to your ear grits."

"If we don't leave right now, I'm pretty sure my lifetime is over." Zenith could see the Shlurp climbing quickly up the starlit hill. He nudged the pouting gargoyle gently with his toe. "Hey, I've got a new deal for you—you stall the thing that's chasing us, and if

we ever return to GrahBhag, you'll get an all-you-can-eat buffet of my grits. Ears, toes, belly button. All yours for the taking."

Kreeble's eyes lit up. She ran her tongue across her lips, imagining the future feast. "I accept your terms." The gargoyle sprinted down the hill to meet the approaching Shlurp. She leapt on top of it and began punching, biting, and clawing at it with a ferocity that shocked Zenith.

"Glad she's on our side," he muttered to Apogee. He hugged his sister tightly and jumped feetfirst into the hole.

Climb

H E FELL UPWARD into the chamber of the foul mouths, landing on his backside but keeping a firm grip on Apogee. Zenith looked up and breathed a sigh of relief. Light streamed down from above them. The brass clasp of the giant bag was still open. The connection to their own world had not been broken.

Although he'd traveled through Dry Mouth again, the voice of Big Mouth was the first he heard. "Bravo, young man! Bravo! I see you have retrieved your sister. Or . . . someone's sister." Then she muttered to Little Mouth, "Looks quite a bit smaller than before, no?"

"I thought none of you could see. What exactly are you looking with?" Zenith jogged over to the wall of snake scales that he'd climbed down at the start of his travels.

"We use language metaphorically, boy," sneered Little Mouth. "Don't be so literal. No one likes a nitpicker of words."

"You'd hate my friend Kreeble, then." Zenith placed Apogee gently on the floor and took off the backpack. He stretched his aching arms and back.

"I think we are getting off track," interjected Big Mouth. "We congratulate you. We are happy to have played a small part in your success and stand ready to assist you once again. For a price."

"Let me guess. You're looking for some more of my blood."

"Your blood or the child's blood. The choice is yours," said Little Mouth, unable to keep the hunger out of her voice.

"You've already paid the price," rasped Dry Mouth from her dusty corner.

"Keep quiet, you!" hissed Little Mouth.

"The blood you spilled at the start of your journey pays for your passage home," continued Dry Mouth. "Don't let these greedy cracks tell you otherwise."

"Thank you," said Zenith. "I thought that might be the case. Otherwise, the bag would be shut."

The three mouths argued among themselves,

but Zenith ignored them. He turned his attention back to the problem at hand—how to climb the wall of scales while carrying Apogee. He pulled the physics textbook out of the backpack and put it aside. "Sorry, sis. I'll get you another copy." He grabbed his pint-size sister and slid her into the backpack, then pulled the twin zippers up around both sides of Apogee's body till they were snugged in under her tiny armpits.

"Ouch, 'Nit!"

"Also, sorry for the tight fit," Zenith replied. He delivered one more apology, though this one was less sincere. "Sorry to be the cause of strife among you three," Zenith said loudly. "But don't worry, you won't be seeing us again. Or tasting our blood."

"Don't be so sure, boy," snickered Little Mouth.

"We can hinder as well as help," added Big Mouth ominously. She retched and disgorged the Shlurp, which rolled across the floor.

Kreeble had definitely done some damage to it. The tight tangle of its hair had partially unraveled and revealed the dark purple heart at the center of the beast. It beat slowly, and with every pulse, black blood oozed onto the floor. But any hope that the terrible thing was about to perish was soon extinguished as it lurched up off its side and teetered toward Zenith and Apogee.

"Squash it," yelled Apogee, and Zenith did as he was told. He grabbed the physics textbook and dropped to his knees as the Shlurp closed the distance between them. He raised the thick book over his head and brought it down on the beast. One. Two. Three times. Then three times more. Then another three times. And though a part of him wanted to keep beating the ghastly thing forever, nine times would have to do. Whether it was dead or not, it wasn't moving. And while it wasn't moving, *they* had better do so.

Apogee must've had the same thought. She wriggled out of the backpack and began climbing the wall on her own. Zenith was at first worried and then relieved as he watched her ascend with amazing skill and speed. Although he now had room for it, he left the bloodied book on top of the terrible thing. He snatched the backpack, grabbed the edge of a snake scale, and hoisted himself off the ground.

The sound of excited sipping caused him to pause. He turned to see a pool of the Shlurp's blood

slowly moving toward the dark corner. "Oh, thank you!" said Dry Mouth between gulps. "This is the first meal I've had in I don't know how long! Not as sweet as Firman blood, but still, delicious!"

"Uh, you're welcome?" Zenith was grateful for the dim light.

"No, *you* are welcome. Welcome to return to GrahBhag whenever you wish! What a feast!"

"Now who's the greedy one!" said Big Mouth.

"Yes! Share with your sisters, Squirt!" demanded Little Mouth.

Dry Mouth didn't respond, and neither did Zenith. He did his best to climb quickly, but the many physical challenges of their escape were taking a toll. They needed to get out of the horrible bag before exhaustion overwhelmed him.

Apogee had stopped near the thread he'd left tethered to the wall. Zenith paused there beside her. He was a pretty good rope climber, but the top of this rope was nowhere near the bag's clasp anymore. When the seam had unraveled during his initial descent, the place where the thread was anchored to the bag's slanted ceiling had shifted dramatically. If they were to climb up it, they would hit a dead end.

How were they going to make it up and over to the opening?

A wicked giggle came from Little Mouth. Zenith looked down and saw that the Shlurp was no longer under the physics book. It was climbing up the wall after them. It was beaten and bedraggled, but it was still coming. A part of him had to admire the dogged determination of the thing. The larger part of him hated its disgusting guts.

Zenith tore his gaze away from the advancing fiend. He had an idea. No time for second guesses. He held the backpack out toward his sister. "Climb in," he said, and Apogee did so with no objection. He tightened the zippers around her as he had before, put it on, and tightened the straps around himself. Apogee grabbed his neck. He grabbed the end of the rope and climbed a little farther up the wall. He gave the opening a long, hard look, took two steps farther up, then came back down one. He slowly turned around so that his back was facing the wall. He gathered up the slack till he was gripping the rope somewhere around the middle of its length. He gave it a hard tug. It seemed secure enough. Zenith looked down. The Shlurp was close. Thirty seconds, maybe less, before it reached them.

"Do it, 'Nit," Apogee said firmly.

"Hold on tight," he replied. Her arms tightened around his neck, her head resting between his shoulder blades.

With as much force as his tired body could muster, Zenith pushed himself off the wall. They swung out into nothing, and for a few dreadful seconds, Zenith was sure he'd misjudged—they were going to be too low. But the rope reached the bottom of its arc and began to swing back up as they approached the bag's opening. Zenith ended up *higher* than he'd expected. His arms smacked into the giant brass clasp at the elbows. He dropped the rope and scrambled madly to get a grip on the opening. He ended up with his face pressed against the cool metal of the clasp, the fingers of his left hand gripping its upper edge, and his right arm slung over the top at the elbow. His fingers could touch the smooth wooden floor of his bedroom but couldn't find anything to grab.

With his last bit of strength, Zenith swung his right leg up, hooked his ankle over the clasp's edge, and hauled his sister and himself up. The bag's opening telescoped down around him as he swung up over its threshold. He landed on the bedroom floor

facedown beside the now normal-size bag. Apogee crawled out of the backpack while he lay there, stepping on top of his head as she did. Zenith muttered a quiet, happy "ow" and decided to stay facedown on the floor. Maybe for the rest of his life.

His life plans were ruined by the Shlurp. Its vile legs came slithering up out of the horrible bag. Before Zenith had a chance to do anything about it, Apogee teetered forward, wielding his baseball bat over her tiny head. The tip of her tongue protruded from between her lips as she brought the bat down squarely onto the Shlurp's body. The odious creature lost its grip on the opening just before Apogee lost her grip on her weapon, and the terrible thing and the bat toppled down into the bag together.

Zenith threw himself on top of the horrible bag, forcing the clasp closed underneath him. And this time, he took the idea of staying on the floor for the rest of his life a little more seriously.

The Missing Shoe

ZENITH WRAPPED HIS bike cable twice around the horrible bag and locked it shut. With that done, he paused and listened. The house was silent. If their parents had been home, they would've come running when they heard the ruckus in his bedroom. They must've been out searching for the two of them. They'd probably gotten the police involved.

Zenith eyed his digital clock. It displayed the date as well as the time. His mouth dropped open. He and Apogee hadn't been gone for two days. According to the clock, they'd only been gone for two hours.

He couldn't believe his luck. Illogically, it was still the same day they'd been pulled into the bag, and their parents were still out. If he acted quickly, he could use the chalk and chalkboard to return Apogee to her proper age, make a devil's bargain for

her silence, and leave their parents none the wiser. Zenith chuckled with the special joy someone feels when they get away with something.

Then he looked at his little sister, and the laughing sputtered and stopped. He got down on his knees, put his hand on her shoulder, then tried to say, "Sorry, Apogee," but his words came out garbled and croaky. Zenith cleared his throat. "I'm sorry, Apogee," he repeated more clearly. "I'm sorry for getting you kidnapped and for almost getting us both killed and for just generally being a crappy brother ever since the accident in Kalikov Park. You were right. I had that all mixed up. You weren't trying to stop me from winning the game. You were trying to stop me from losing my life. I wish I could revise and rewrite the way I've behaved, but there's not enough room on the chalkboard."

"It's okay, 'Nit." Apogee leaned forward, kissed him on the cheek, and hugged him. Zenith exhaled and hugged her back. After a moment, Apogee pulled away and gave him one of her stares. "Now change me back."

"Yes. Absolutely. Your wish is my command. Your next *hundred* wishes are my command."

He pulled the sparkly chalk from his pants and patted the pocket of his hoodie where he'd stowed the chalkboard. But it was empty.

Was he misremembering? Had he put it inside the backpack instead? He searched every pocket in the pack three times over, then dumped everything out onto the floor. No chalkboard.

Where's the chalkboard? he thought. "Where's the chalkboard?" he asked Apogee. "Where's the chalkboard?!?" he screamed to no one in particular. He fell back on his butt as his feet shot out from underneath him. He scratched his scar furiously and stared at his shoes.

Something was wrong. Not having the chalkboard was wrong, but something else was wrong as well. His shoes were wrong. How were they wrong?

He thought that one of them had come off. When they'd crashed at the Collectory, it'd flown past his face in a green blur, and he'd never stopped to retrieve it. And yet there were two shoes on his two feet. A lot of things he'd thought were impossible had happened over the last couple of days (or last couple of hours), but he still had a hard time believing in self-replicating shoes.

All at once, he stopped scratching. His eyes went wide. "The shoe never came off. The green thing that flew by my face was the chalkboard." He didn't want it to be true, but he knew it was. In the confusion of the crash and the rush to escape, he'd left the chalkboard inside the horrible bag, and now his sister was stuck at the wrong age and he was stuck being the older sibling.

And then he was struck by his younger sibling. Apogee picked up one of his dirty socks and threw it at him. "Fix me, 'Nit," she demanded. Zenith opened his mouth, hoping his brain would find some way to explain things and got a mouthful of sock as his reward. "Fix me!"

He heard the distant but unmistakable sound of the front door opening. "Zenith? Apogee?" called his mother. "We're home!" his father chimed in.

"Fix me, fix me, fix me!" his sister wailed. She began beating her tiny fists on his shoulder.

Zenith resumed his nervous scratching as Apogee screamed her tiny lungs out. He heard his parents running toward his room. The bedroom door swung open, and his mom rushed into the room. "Zenith! Apogee! Are you okay?" Her panicked gaze fell on

Zenith's face for only a moment before she saw the four-year-old crying beside him.

His mom rushed forward and opened her arms. "Oh, Geegee, what's wrong?" She scooped Apogee up off the floor and held her tight. After a moment comforting her daughter, she confronted her son. "Shame on you! Just sitting there while your baby sister cries." She turned on her heel and stormed out of the room past his dad, who stood just inside the doorway.

His dad let out an exhausted sigh. "When you're ready, come to the den. We're going to have yet another talk about what it means to be the big brother. And just how long you'll be grounded this time." He turned and left.

Zenith sat on the floor, shocked into silence and totally confused. He sat that way for a very long time.

Summer Fun

THE BAG GROANED. Or at least that's how it sounded to Zenith from the other side of the door. When it fell on the front porch, he could have sworn that it groaned. Zenith opened the door, and there stood Kevin Churl, massaging one foot. "Dropped my bag on it."

Zenith rolled his eyes. "Come in, klutz."

Kevin stepped inside, moving his duffel bag from the porch to the entryway floor. "You up for a little blacktop hockey?" Kevin gestured toward the hockey stick poking out from the partially unzipped bag. "Safer than the winter variety. No ice for us to fall through."

Zenith regarded him and the bag doubtfully.

"C'mon! It's a gorgeous day."

Zenith looked out the front door. The sun was a wonderful yellow, and the sky was a healthy shade of blue. The birds in the trees were all bird-size.

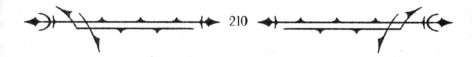

"I don't know. I should really keep an eye on my baby sister."

"For heaven's sake, Zenith! Get out of the house for a little while," called his mother from down the hall. Zenith and Kevin walked to the large archway that opened onto the living room. His mom sat hunkered down on the sofa, her eyes on the Sunday paper. Apogee sat beside her, coloring a drawing on the coffee table. "I appreciate how protective you've become, but I'm fully capable of watching Apogee all on my own." His mom reached out and ruffled her daughter's hair.

"You'll put her down for her nap?" asked Zenith.

"As soon as she finishes her latest masterpiece." Apogee paused her work and yawned. His mom put down her newspaper. "Or maybe sooner. Go on, you two, get out of here."

Zenith walked with Kevin to the cul-de-sac at the end of their block. He could scarcely believe he was allowed to leave the house. His dad had extended his summertime detention by only two days. Of course, he'd been punished for making his baby sister cry, not for turning his teenaged sister into a baby.

Zenith had worried about the bag being moved

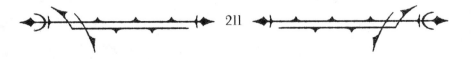

while they were inside it, had worried that they would come out in a strange place. The bag was exactly where they left it, but they'd *still* emerged in a strange place—a world where Zenith was and always had been the older sibling. During the days that followed, it became clear that nobody besides Zenith remembered the version of reality in which Apogee had been fourteen instead of four.

Well, nobody but Apogee herself. She remembered quite clearly, and was furious at Zenith. She didn't care that he'd changed her age to save her from the Wurm. She wasn't sure they understood the purpose of the Merging, and truth be told, neither was Zenith. She didn't want to hear how, in his panic, he'd mistaken the slate for his shoe. She just wanted things fixed. But as much as he would've liked to have his big sister back, Zenith could think of nothing that would do the trick, short of returning to GrahBhag and retrieving the magic chalkboard. They'd barely escaped with their lives the first time.

A few of the neighborhood kids were waiting for them at the end of the block. Zenith smiled as Kevin handed out hockey sticks and argued amiably with the rest of them over who would be on whose team.

The one good thing that'd happened in the last couple weeks was his new friendship with Kevin. After what he and Apogee had gone through in GrahBhag, apologizing to Kevin for what had occurred on the pond in Kalikov Park didn't seem like such a big deal. He also apologized for taking so long to apologize. Kevin had shrugged, and said, "Better late than never." They'd been hanging out ever since. When Zenith wasn't busy watching over Apogee.

Zenith spent a carefree hour playing hockey. They were all having a good time, goofing around and laughing. The score was tied, but no one really cared who won. Still, when Zenith suddenly froze up and failed to block a slow shot on their goal, his team grumbled.

He didn't seem to notice. He turned toward Kevin with a wild look in his eyes. "I need to go home." He dropped his stick and ran down the street without further explanation. Both teams groused as he left.

Zenith burst through the front door and headed straight for his room. As he'd once written on the missing chalkboard, Zenith now knew exactly where to find Apogee at any given moment. And yet he

still had a hard time believing what he saw when he opened his bedroom door.

Apogee sat on the floor, grappling with the paper clip she'd inserted into the lock he'd placed on the horrible bag, the tip of her tongue protruding from between her lips.

It seemed that no matter how high the shelf or how dark the corner he hid the bag in, she found it. Luckily the latest lock had held, but she would pick it eventually. It was a skill she had in common with his friend Kreeble.

Apogee didn't stop nor even look up as Zenith crossed the room. He picked up the picture lying next to her. It was a drawing of an older Apogee riding a large raven. The black bird's emerald scarf was in her one hand, a small glowing chalkboard in the other.

Zenith sat down next to his sister. "You're not going to stop, are you?"

"No." Apogee leaned away from him.

"I don't mean just now. I mean ever. You're never going to give up trying to open it."

"No." She switched hands but kept fiddling with the paper clip.

"I can't keep watch over you every second, Apogee. Even if I give up the idea of having any fun this summer, what happens when I go back to school in the fall?"

No answer this time. But he didn't need one. Zenith had the answer. He reached out and stilled Apogee's hand with his own. She gave him one of her withering gazes.

"So we're going back. Not today, not until we've had some time to plan. But we're going back inside the horrible bag."

Apogee's mouth widened into a smile. "Really?"

Zenith leaned back on his elbows; his chin met his chest. "Really."

Apogee giggled. Zenith groaned.

And a faint chuckle came from inside the horrible bag.

ACKNOWLEDGMENTS

For their help with this horrible tale, my heartfelt thanks to:

Eric Geron, who offered nothing but wisdom and encouragement, even when this book was in its ugliest duckling phase.

Alex Hirsch, whom I respect as a storyteller and cherish as a friend. His insightful questions and comments were invaluable, as always.

Tracy Royce, my wife and partner. An excellent writer in her own right, she lent her keen instincts, critical eye, and precision with language to this tale.

John Goldsmith, my animation agent and longtime friend, who saw the potential in this project even after I told him I thought it should be a book first, and did everything in his power to make that happen.

Rubin Pfeffer, my literary agent and fast friend, who has been so kind and generous with his immense knowledge, good taste, and great instincts. He steered this story out into the world and found it the proper home.

Alex Wolfe and Rob Valois, my editors, and the rest of the Penguin Workshop team, including Mary Claire Cruz, Shara Hardeson, Caroline Press, Ana Deboo, Vivian Kirklin, and Jessica Nevins. They have treated this story with respect and enthusiasm, and wisely guided it into its final form. I am honored to be publishing it with them.

M. S. Corley, for applying his immense artistic talents to create a fantastic cover and giving us our first glimpses of the creatures inside the horrible bag.

And Erik Lee, who casually suggested I write my own original book series, as if it were just that simple. When I was done scoffing silently to myself, my next thought was, *Why not?* My subsequent thoughts formed the kernel of this story.